TALES OF KINGS AND GLORY

A WICKED PLACE

TRISTEN SNYDER

A dozen men worked the deck of the ship in total silence. The morning fret speckled their black coats with water droplets. Beneath their consuming hoods were faces scarred beyond recognition—and within those faces, a pair of eyes filled with madness waiting insufferably to be unleashed. Peering into the myst at the bow of the ship stood a very different man. He clasped behind his back, his red coat reaching far below them. His mismatched blue and green eyes boredly watched as the shape of the approaching docks began appearing through the myst. Hushed words and quiet replies whispered at this sight. Despite the calm waters, the cloaked men scurried around the ship at the speed of only a man in fear for his life. The whispers silenced to only the sounds of water lapping against the hull, boots scurrying about the deck, and sails flapping in the wind. Fastly approaching the pier, their anchor broke the quietness with a loud splash. Four of the cloaked men jumped the span between the cog and the pier roped in the small ship. The gangplank crashed down as the crew scrambled to get it down in the red man's wake. The cloaked men followed the red man across the plank like beat dogs, and the ones tying the ship off backed away in fear as his first boot stepped onto the pier.

Walking down the gloomy docks, the red man looked at the shadows of the surrounding ships. Most were poor fishing barges, barely capable of making their daily voyages. A single carrack from the mainland stuck out sorely against the decrepit barges. The red man knew it to be the ship he was pursuing.

A reddish light crept towards him, eerily turning the mysty air an orangish colour. The Red continued towards the approaching light. When the light finally emerged from the haze, he was met by an old fisherman. Deeming the scraggly, ageing angler to be no threat, he clasped his hands behind his back rather than upon the hilt of his sabre.

"Who might y'all be?" The fisherman rasped, poking his head in front of the lantern to get a better look at the lot before him.

"Travellers," the red man said, looking into his eyes.

The cloaked men spread apprehensively in a semi-circle around the stranger, their heads looking down or away from the geezer.

"My-o, I've never seen so many visitors in one day! What brings y'all to our little 'sland?" The fisherman asked, combing his beard with greasy fingers.

"We are looking for somebody. A dwarf."

The fisherman twirled his beard around his pointer finger, "Hm… Er… Tavern most like. Ain't many places else to go 'ere. Tis not a big-"

In the middle of his sentence, one of the cloaked men lashed out with a dagger concealed in his sleeve. The lantern shattered as it crashed onto the deck. The man gurgled, bubbles of blood forming at the slit in his throat.

The cloaked man lashed out again. The fisherman stumbled backwards, collapsing next to the shattered lantern, its wick still burning.

Pouncing onto his prey, the cloaked man stabbed him again and again. Another joins him, then another, all rabidly sinking their blades into the man's flesh. Finally the lantern's flame blew out.

"Enough!" The red man snapped, and the cloaked men scurried away from the bloody pulp like kicked dogs. *'Soon you won't be so damn... unstable.'*

The man continued down the pier until he reached a mildewed building; a sign above the door read *The Trout's Stout*. Jerking the door jammed by rust open, he felt the warm, musty air before even entering. The cloaked men followed the red man in and retreated to the empty corners of the room. Between the troves of anglers' daughters who had nothing to resort to but selling themselves, the drinks flowing to loosen up traveller's coin pouches, the creaking and moaning from upstairs, and the scent of fish and cheap perfume, the red man could barely tell it apart from a brothel. In these carnal affairs, the red man had no interest. Instead, he headed straight towards the dwarf seated across the room.

The red man sat down across the table from the Dwarf and silently observed his peculiar appearance. He was fashioned in all black, every inch of his body concealed. Upon his face was a black crow's-beak mask with tinted glass eyelets, and upon his head was a hat with a gambler crown and a brim as wide as his shoulders.

The two stared for a long time into each other's unsettling faces.

"Do you want something?" The Dwarf finally said, his voice muffled in the mask.

"Yes. You are Yashin, are you not?"

The Dwarf took off his hat before he unbuckled his crow mask, then set them both on the table. Beneath the mask was an even stranger sight. The Dwarf's skin was dark grey; his hairs a grey so light that against his skin they might have looked falsely white to somebody less observant; and his eyes were two glossy black voids filled with colourful specs that were reminiscent of the night sky. If the red man was at all surprised, he showed no sign of it.

"A Rumaasi Dwarf," the red man said in fascination. "They say your kind has conquered death?"

Yashin chuckled and shook his head. "You put it as if it were some sort of achievement. Aye, I may succumb not to ageing nor ailment, but that is only one of the less adverse consequences of this curse."

The red man was intrigued. "So your kind can still perish?"

"Very much so. We are still vulnerable to the blade—and worse yet—in constant peril of the sun. If my skin were ever to see the sun's rays, it would turn me to stone."

"You speak in the singular… Am I mistaken for there being others?"

"There were others… If there is any other than I, it is seldom few. The past millennium has not been merciful. And those who tried to bear children only begot tragedy." Yashin's black eyes wandered away with a hint of sadness in them.

The red man cocked his head. "In what way?"

Yashin's eyes snapped back to the red man. "I know you did not come here for me to tell you about an ancient curse."

The man affirmed the Dwarf's assertion with a nod. "I am looking for the Mask."

"Mask?" Yashin feigned. "I'm not sure I know what you are referencing?"

"A bird told me you did."

Yashin conceded with a small smile. "A literal bird, I take it?"

"Will you tell me where it is?"

Yashin thought carefully for a long minute before he spoke. "Aye. But before I divulge to you this information, you must heed the story behind this accursed *Mask* you are after—the story of Mancipus."
The red man leaned back in his chair and nodded.

◈ Chapter Two

Yashin stood at the decks, looking out across the great Marmedius Sea. The sun was slowly receding below the waters that went beyond horizons, setting the sky and sea ablaze with vivid shades of reds and oranges and yellows. A lighthouse stood proudly on one isle of the small archipelago, but its light had not been lit for a long while. It was across this sea that he was to flee, away from the Flouvern Empire and to the northern empire of the Kraftvollenreich where he would hopefully be safe. When he came to the Empire, it was to escape one threat to his life, but another quickly took its place.

"You there!" A hoarse voice shouted behind him. Yashin ignored the voice in hopes it would just pass—yet it called again: "Half-man!"

Slowly waddling to turn around, he found a squad of men dressed in *Lorica Segmentata* towering above him, torches in hand. Legionaries.

"May I help you, my good Dekarchos?"

"Do not call me Dekarchos, half-man! Thou shall refer to all Legionaries ranks in the holy tongue!"

"Pardon me, *Decanus*… I mean no offence… I often forget the patricians have forsaken their own tongue for the… holy language."

"Why doth thee conceal thy face half-man?" The Decanus questioned.

Having been wearing so much clothing for many years, Yashin often forgot it was even on him. "I must keep my body wrapped. Without my protection, I would perish."

"It would seem to me you are a criminal!" The Decanus concluded. His nasty scowl then morphed into a sadistic smile. "Under the directive of Emperor Peuri, all non-human criminals are to be apprehended and sent to assist the war effort."

"I have committed no crime. The courts will find that," Yashin said, mostly trying to assure himself.

"You will see no court, half-man. The war office has decreed that any non-humans under suspicion of any crime shall be imprisoned at the discretion of the Cohorets Vigilum."

"First you took our homes from us, then stole the fruits of our labour, and now you are imprisoning us without ground or trial?!" Yashin asked in disbelief.

The Decanus spat on Yashin, though he did not feel it through the various layers that covered him. "Be glad I am not killing thee where thou stand! Your filth does not belong in this world. Alas, Emperor Peuri spared your kind so that you may pay us reparations."

"Ahh so it is coin you desire, my friend?" This would not be the first time he found himself being extorted by a human.

The Decanus and his men laughed in sinister unison.

"... in the form of labour until the day you die. And even then, you shall not have repaid what you have stolen from us."

His plans, like the sky and sea before him, were in flames.

*****

Yashin woke up on his hard wooden bed, the ship slowly rocking back and forth. He sat up in his bunk and looked out of the cell. Rays of sunlight beamed through the ship's grates; despite none directly beaming into his cell, he still always kept his face wrapped just in case. It was a small compartment in the ship, with just barely enough room for a bunk and a shit-bucket in the corner.

Seconds after sitting up, he heard footsteps descending the passageway. A figure silently climbed down from the rack above. He was a thin young-man, dressed similarly to Yashin in fading black clothing. Two large cheekbones stuck out predominantly, his face skinny from years of malnutrition. Yashin learned his name to be Imbert. Believing it to be morning chow, the cellmates grabbed their bowls and waited at the grated door.

In the cell across the passageway, a creature emerged from the shadows with its bowl in hand. It was like that of a Goblin, with its greenish-brown skin, jutting lower jaw, and pointy ears. But contrasting the short and scrawny Goblins, this creature towered nigh six feet tall and was of large build.

All three nervously took a step back when two men who stopped in front of their cells turned out not to be the two cooks; in their place were two Legionaries.

"When we open your cells, you will exit slowly and make way atop deck," One Legionary barked to the prisoners. "Do you understand, degenerates?"

"Aye," Yashin affirmed, his voice muffled by his mask.

Imbert nodded, and the creature made an affirmative sounding grunt.

The same Legionary fumbled through a few of the keys on his ring before choosing one. He unlocked the cell door and violently slid it open. Yashin and Imbert did not dare move until the Legionaries backed away from their cell and turned to the creature.

"Get back!" The other Legionaries shouted at it right before banging on the metal bars.

Yashin cautiously exited his cell and slipped behind the Legionaries, Imbert following at his heels. A few feet away from the soldiers, the two shuffled faster away from them and up a ladder. Emerging on the top deck, clouds brewed above, rays of sun only intermittently piercing through the gaps. The sails and rigging flapped rapidly in the wind, and Yashin wished he could have felt the breeze on his skin. A Legionary snaps Yashin out of his trance, pointing to the starboard while screaming "What's the hold up?! Onto the boats!"

Hung from a crane off the side of the ship was a large dinghy, a pair of Legionaries in it at the oars. Reaching the edge, Yashin found the gap between the ship and the dinghy was too great for his stubby legs. He stood at the edge, thinking there was nothing he could do but wait to get screamed at. Then he felt a pair of large hands pick him up by the waist and gently set him into the boat. Spinning around to see his helper, the creature smiled and nodded. He took a seat at the bow, and Imbert sat across from the Dwarf, his back to two Imperial oarsmen. Then the creature sat next to Imbert.

Then came another man, his hair as black as water on a moonless night, dressed in dark grey clothes, and standing too proud for having been a prisoner. Trying to keep up was a Dwarf, his hair ginger and beard a couple inches long. The man got into the boat easily enough and sat at the stern. Like Yashin the Dwarf found his legs too short, but with no giant creature to help him in, the Dwarf could only try to jump the gap. He gave it a valiant try, but still caught his foot on the dinghy's hull and landed on his face. As he tried to get back on his feet, the crane operator abruptly dropped the dinghy into the water. He fell forward again and his head slammed into the starboard hull. The two Legionaries began rowing, and the Dwarf dizzily crawled next to the grey-clad man.

Yashin took in the bay that surrounded them. Besides the narrow mouth, snow-capped mountains surrounded them on all sides. Coniferous trees stood high anywhere there were not steep rocky faces, fighting one another to for the little light that the cloudy skies provided, creating sinister black forest floors.

He studied the creature seated before him. "What are you?"

It shrugged. "I am Goreg… Of the Makrag Heights."

"You speak Flouvic?" Imbert asked, surprised.

Goreg nodded his head. "It was taught to me many year ago." With those words, his face turned dark and sombre.

"But what are you?" Yashin asked again. "I have been alive since before the Empires and I have never seen a creature such as yourself until now."

Goreg shrugged. "Don't know."

"Well where are you from?"

"Makrag Heights."

While he could speak language and show empathy, the creature lacked knowledge of geography or ecology, Yashin concluded.

Then the creature began speaking. "My people have long told tales of us being slaves in big mountains. But long ago we fled big mountains and settled Makrag Heights."

Yashin nodded, trying to decipher any usable information out of it.

The boat headed towards a settlement built upon a thin peninsula, Flovourn colours flying high on a tall flagpole. Small stubby houses made of rocks and clay were erected in seemingly unplanned locations, and a fortified Castrum built with glorious Flouvern architecture was at the end of the peninsula. Around the settlement on land was a large wooden palisade, hastily fashioned from the trees that once populated the peninsula.

A second boat was quickly launched behind the first. When they neared the docks, a man scurried to the edge of the pier, dressed in a white tunic, beige trousers, and a red cape that was draped around his shoulders. He impatiently tapped his foot as the dinghies inched near. After what felt like forever with the man watching them, they pulled up to the docks and slowly unboarded. The other boat pulled up shortly after the first. They had loaded this one with Legionaries and two prisoners: a redhead man with wild hair, and a scrawny woman with a weasel-like face.

Only after everybody had disembarked the dinghies did the man speak.

"I am Legate Justinian Carissius. You have arrived earlier than we had expected, and as such our Praetor, Severus Claudus, has not yet returned. In the meantime… Welcome to Mancipus."

"Mancipus? Where the fuck are we?" The man dressed in grey asked brazenly.

Legate Justinian smiled sadly. "We are on a chain of islands far off the eastern coast of our Kraft adversaries."

"I thought they were sending me to assist in the war effort?" The man asked snarkily.

"You are, my friend. Our emperor, the awe-full Peuri, has sent us here to claim the treasures of this island." Justinian tugged on his cape to adjust the clasp, shaped like a torch with its flames shooting out in the shape of an eagle—the sigil of the Flouvern under Emperor Peuri I's rule.

"I was looking forward to killin' me some Krafts or Vorons."

"I am sorry to disappoint you. I hope your time here in Mancipus will sate your appetite for adventure. Might I ask, what is your name?"

"I am Remus Schneffer," the man proclaimed.

"And the rest of you all might be..?" Justinian asked.

The other Dwarf began, "I am-"

The redhead man cut him off, bowing as he said, "Falnon of Erysinia."

Again, the Dwarf opened his mouth to speak, only to be cut off by his Rumaasi counterpart.

"Yashin."

"I am Nurin Uvazebûrzan," the other Dwarf finally managed.

Justinian looked to the last two. He finally realised after a long awkward silence they weren't planning on introducing themselves. Scratching at his lengthy blonde hair, he spoke, "Onto the next matter of importance."

He began down the docks, only to stop when he looked over his shoulder and saw none were following. "This way!"

Justinian stopped before a sizable building positioned right on the docks. He stopped at the door and turned around with a smile.

"This is our little town's tavern. Should you fulfil your duties to our Empire with time to spare, you may come here as you please. It is in need of a tavern-keep, which will-"

With one hand on his hip and the other raised in a fist, Falnon enthusiastically interrupted him, "I will take the position!"

"*Tsk, tsk.*" Yashin shook his head. "I have extensive experience running such establishments."

Justinian frowned as he looked back and forth between the two indecisive. "Perhaps we should take a vote?"

Yashin and Falnon glared at one another before nodding to accept the proposal.

"All for Falnon of Erysinia!" Justinian proclaimed.

Remus raised his hand and smiled at Falnon, followed by the woman. Falnon's smirk gave way to a frown as none of the others voted for him.

"And all for Yashin!"

Imbert and Nurin raised their hands for him.

The group looked to Goreg to break the tie. The beast only gave them a shrug.

"Perhaps we should flip a coin?" Nurin suggested.

Justinian pulled a bronze coin from his tunic pocket and fiddled with it. "What sides shall you choose?"

"Heads!" Falnon jumped to claim.

"Tails is acceptable," Yashin confirmed.

With a flick of his thumb, Justinian sent the coin flying high into the air. Justinian reached out for the coin but sent it bouncing out of his hand. Imberts hand shot out and he clenched his fist around it. For a moment it felt like the world went still, except for an almost unperceivable twitching of Imbert's fingers that clutched the coin. The man stuck out the back of his other hand and slapped the coin down onto it. The coin was on tails.

◈ Chapter Three

The Foghouse Tavern was empty, other than Imbert sipping his beer every several minutes. Yashin was in the back corner washing dirty mugs, which the previous caretaker seemed to have never cleaned. The tavern was a mess, everything covered in a thick layer of dust, spiderwebs spanning between almost every object, and nothing having been kept tidied. Unsurprisingly, the bed he had found himself using in the loft was sweat stained and smelled rancid. But it was arguably a better arrangement than the bunkhouses the others were in.

The sound of an opening door alerted Yashin. Moments later, he heard the faint sound of two men speaking to one another. Waddling to the front of the tavern, he saw the two men: Falnon and Remus.

"How do you plan on doing that?" Falnon asked as they walked towards the bar.

"I don't exactly know yet," Remus said, and the two men took their seats.

Yashin pulled out two mugs from beneath the counter: a clean one for Remus, and a dirty one for Falnon. "What would you like to drink?"

"Anything will do," Remus told him.

Falnon scratched his stubble chin. "What wines do you have?"

Yashin laughed. His voice muffled and distorted by his mask, he informed the man, "We got grog and some ale."

Falnon's face soured with disgust. "Ale will have to do."

"Ten coppers each," Yashin said as he stuck out his palm.

"Ten? That's half the week's allowance!" Remus cried.

Yashin curled his fingers to signal payment. "Stocks are low. What else are you planning to spend it on, anyhow?"

The men's faces soured as they reluctantly counted their coins and handed over ten coppers each. After they paid him, Yashin pulled a ceramic jug out from beneath the counter. Uncorking the bottle unleashed the stench of soured wine and ginger, and he poured a cloudy brown liquid into Remus' cup. As Yashin re-corked the bottle and returned it beneath the counter, Remus tried a sip, and his face indicated it was not as bad as one might've thought. Then Yashin procured a pitcher of ale. Unbeknownst to his soon-to-be victim, Yashin had found this pitcher sitting out on the bar when he first entered the establishment. After receiving his drink, Falnon took a sip and gagged. His face hidden behind his dark mask, Yashin's victim could not see him grinning.

"Enjoy your drinks," Yashin told them before he returned to scrubbing mugs. Over the soft sound of scrubbing, Yashin could overhear all of the men's conversation.

First spoke Falnon; "We don't know when the Praetor is going to return. If you plan on doing it, you shouldn't wait."

"It should be easy enough; we've both seen that he walks around the place without guard," Remus told him.

"It's like he forgets this is a penal colony," Falnon laughed.

Remus hushed himself some, but still not enough to not be heard by the Dwarf. "Estren will lure him away from prying eyes this eve. She will petition him for a bunkhouse only for womenfolk. Maybe make him think he'll get a good prodding in. When they're alone, I'll do it."

Yashin heard a loud gulping sound followed by the slamming of a mug on the counter.

"Not going to drink yours?" He could hear Remus ask.

"It seems my palette disagrees with ale," Falnon told him. "Let us get out of this shithole?"

Yashin heard the two men stand up from their chairs. He waited for them to slam the door before he stopped cleaning and waddled back to the bar and emptied the half-drunk ale back into the pitcher.

" I need you to do something," he shouted across the bar to the man lurking in the far corner.

"Yes?" Imbert asked.

"Watch Justinian. If that Remus tries anything, do what you do," Yashin ordered.

Imbert nodded and slipped out of the Foghouse. As Imbert left, Yashin saw through the cracked door and noted that the sun was setting. Once again, he retreated to the back and continued to clean and organise.

After some time of working on getting the Foghouse shaped up, Yashin heard the door creak open again. Remus and three Legionaries entered the tavern. Yashin quickly grabbed four mugs and set them out for the men as they sat down.

"Good thing I caught 'im. Without me, the Legate might not 'ave been breathing right now," Remus boasted.

"Mm. Perhaps," one Legionary grunted as he took off his crested helmet and set it on the table. A Centurion, Yashin knew from his helmet.

"What can I get you all to drink?" Yashin asked the men, pretending to be uninterested in their conversation.

"Anythin' with alcohol," the Legionary next to the Centurion told him. He pulled the pitcher of grog out from under the table and poured them all drinks. Then the Legionary asked, "How much?"

"Ten coppers," Remus remarked bitterly.

Yashin smiled. "Legionaries get half off."

The men happily paid, and after setting the coin into a lockbox bolted to the counter, he began entering the numbers into his books.

"Shoulda just let the freak assassinate him," the Centurion told Remus. "Justinian is unfit to be Legate. And I would put coin on me being the next Legate if he were to be taken out."

"And then I could replace you as Centurion," the man next to said.

"You wish, Marcellus!" the final Legionary replied.

"Well there ain't no way it would be you, Junus," Marcellus prodded.

"Say, you got any idea who the assassin was?" The Centurion asked Remus.

He shook his head. "He was wearing some balatro mask."

Finished recording his new numbers, Yashin closed his books and set them aside. He waddled around the counter and headed towards the door.

"Where ya going, barkeep?" Marcellus asked.

Stepping out of the tavern, Yashin replied, "I have important business I must tend to."

Like an otherworlder hiding beneath the floorboards from the Imperials, the moon peeked through the cracks of ever looming clouds. Between two bunkhouses, brushes smouldered, red embers nibbling away at them and threatening to relight with every gust. Yashin made haste to the Castrum. Torch fire lit up the building like when mount Pyron erupted and set the entire city ablaze. Flickers of this great beacon glanced the whipping colours of the Empire, flying high on the flagpole behind the compound. The main wing of the Castrum ran parallel to the camp and stood two stories tall. Flanking the sides of the main wing were two connecting single-story wings reaching out towards the camp. Bridging the gap between the two wings to form a perfect square was a defensive wall, a large iron bar gate set in the centre with two sentries guarding it.

When Yashin reached the gate, he told them, "I must speak with the Legate."

"Legate Justinian is busy. Come back tomorrow, Dwarf."

"I cannot. I have important information about the assassin.

The Legionary thought for some time before concluding, "I shall escort you to the Legate. We'll see if he wishes to speak to you."

This Legionary opened the large steel gate and ushered the Dwarf in. Within the courtyard was a forge, and operating the grindstone was a peculiar giant. At first sight Yashin thought it was a tree, but the wooden behemoth was in fact an animate being. Thick, bark-covered wood weaved around a glowing crystalline core, and thin root-like strands held its joints together. The golem turned its head towards Yashin, its eyeholes glowed dimly as the crystal's light made it up its hollow body. Then it went back to grinding a sword.

"How'd that get here?" Yashin inquires.

A deep rumbling radiates from the golem: *BadroOon*.

"Just another abomination they sent here to serve us. Just as yourself," the Legionary spat. "Half decent smith, the thing actually happens to be."

At the other side of the courtyard was a large pair of double-doors. The Legionary opened it for Yashin and told him, "In ya go, Dwarf."

Within the double doors was the grand hall, with a curule seat sat at the end and a colonnade on either side. The Legionary pushed the Dwarf forward and marched him up a staircase, going up to the gallery above the colonnade. From there, the man led Yashin down a tight hallway. Yashin passed a door from which he heard Justinian's muffled voice inside, "-won't speak, you shall force me to use less pleasant methods."

"Stop there," the Legionary ordered.

Yashin halted and dared not move. Just behind his back, he heard the Legionary knock on the door.

The door opened and Justinian asked, "What is it?"

"Legate Justinian, this Dwarf claims to have information about your attacker."

"You may return to your post, Legionary," Justinian told him.

Yashin heard the man turn to leave. Then he turned himself around and waddled into Justinian's office. Inside Imbert was tied to a chair before Justinian's desk, on which sat an eerie grinning mask, the swirling red and green paint cracking and chipping—Imbert's mask.

Justinian returned to his seat across from Imbert. "What is it you wish to tell me about our friend Imbert here?"

Yashin slowly walked across the office, pulled up another chair next to Imbert, and leaned in before answering. "I sent Imbert to follow you."

"Excuse me?!" Justinian exclaimed. He stared in shock for a minute, seemingly unsure what to do, before finally standing from his chair and shouting, "Legionaries! Legionaries!"

"Sit down." Yashin prompted. "Do you really believe I would admit to such if it was ill intended?"

Justinian glared at him suspiciously, yet curiously. "What was your intent, then?"

"Sit down." Yashin repeated.

Justinian cautiously sat back down.

"I sent him not as an assassin, rather a… guardian. You see-"

Four guards burst into the room. "Legate!" One reports.

"Your service is no longer required, Legionary," Yashin notifies them.

"You do not command us, Dwarf!" The guard cursed before looking to Justinian for orders.

Justinian looked to Yashin.

Yashin stared at Justinian.

Justinian looked back to the guard, who was still looking at him.

"You may… return to your post…" Justinian ordered with uncertainty.

The guards hesitantly turned around and left.

Justinian opened his mouth to say something, but Yashin cut him off; "As I was saying, the other prisoners were the ones whom were conspiring against you. We overheard the prisoner Remus conspiring to lead you into a trap and kill you. So I sent Imbert here to see that it didn't happen."

"And why should I believe you are looking out for my well being? After all, I am your captor."

"Remus believes it is in his best interest to have you killed before the Praetor arrives. I think we can agree such is in neither of our interests. There is no getting off this island except for by Imperial ship. I believe it safe to assume the assassination of an Imperial—especially a high ranking one as yourself—would be met with every last one of us hung from the neck. And even if my fellow prisoners were to seize control of this camp, your compatriots would undoubtedly exterminate this entire camp. Is that what happened to the previous occupants?"

Before Justinian could answer, Yashin continued — "I believe it is in my best interest to have you as my ally."

"Ally? What are you on about?"

"I can gather intelligence on the prisoners. Just as I did Remus' plot on your life. Furthermore, I can keep them preoccupied… distracted… pacified… But I would require some of my assets from the mainland, as well as some… leeway."

Justinian contemplated for a long time. "What do you need?"

*****

Imbert sat on the stool on the other side of the bar from Yashin. Besides the two of them, the Foghouse was empty. After swaying Justinian, Yashin and Imbert waited until curfew before returning to the tavern. Doors bolted and their scheming safe from unfriendly ears, Yashin spoke to Imbert for the first time.

"Had it been a different man, I couldn't have saved you from swinging by the neck. How did you get caught?"

Imbert's head drooped down in shame. "I lost sight of Justinian after the woman led him into an empty bunkhouse. I heard a loud noise and believed Remus was inside. As I went through a window, Remus spotted me and shouted."

"And how'd you get *caught*?" Yashin inquired.

"I ran for the bushes, but they burst into flames. Then Remus and some others circled around me."

Yashin nodded his head in thought. "A mage, Remus must be. That makes this situation even more complicated."

Imbert stared at him with an ashamed face.

"I do not blame you for what happened. I think we may have found ourselves in an even better position yet. Go get some sleep, my friend."

Imbert nodded and got up from his stool. The young man left the Foghouse, and Yashin headed to what seemed to be a closet behind the counter. He opened the narrow door and descended into what hid below.

◈ Chapter Four

The sound of the door swinging open and slamming into the wall woke Yashin. Getting out of bed, he waddled to the balcony of the loft that looked into the tavern. Three Legionaries were wandering down below and searching the room.

"Can I help you?" Yashin called to them.

The soldiers looked up, somewhat surprised. One called, "There you are. You are to report to the docks. *Immediately*." Then the three left the Foghouse.

As he remained dressed at all times, Yashin slowly climbed down the ladder, the gaps between each step barely short enough for his legs to reach. One step at a time, he carefully descended. His foot barely setting down on the floorboards, a voice screamed behind him.

"Make haste, halfman!"

He jumped and stumbled back a little, but caught his footing at the last moment. He mumbled to himself in anger, "Umânkaszâd slônc!"

Turning around, he was met with a Legionary snarling at him. As Yashin waddled across the room, complying with the orders as best he could with his stubby legs, the Legionary stormed across the room with long strides. The two beings met, the man snarling down at Yashin and Yashin returning his stare, his look of disgust hidden beneath his dark mask. The man raised his hand and opened his mouth, but before he could act a voice called out.

"Make haste, the Praetor is nearing!" Legate Justinian commanded.

The Legionary froze for a few seconds, then slowly lowered his hand. Grinding his teeth he faced about and marched out of the tavern. Justinian remained in the doorway, nodding at Yashin with a sad smile. Some men have good in them, Yashin thought. But a Dwarf cannot rely on their sympathy.

Following not too far behind the Legate, Yashin made his way to the neighbouring docks. Lined up side by side were all the prisoners, with guards posted on their flanks and lined behind them. He passed Remus, Falnon, Estren, Nurin, and Goreg, until he reached Imbert at the end and stood beside him. He trusted Imbert. No—*trust* was the wrong word; a Human could never be trusted. Imbert was *loyal*.

Legionaries and prisoners alike waited without a word; the only sounds were the waves breaking harshly against the stony shores,and the wind howling through the woods. Then footsteps as a group of men disembarked a rowboat and landed on the docks. Four Legionaries marched down the docks, surrounding in perfect alignment a clearly important man. His tunic was blacker than the cast iron laurel wreath on his head, and his black enameled breastplate was almost as hidden against it as the crown was in his short black hair. The only feature of his livery not black was the white-silver sigil spanning across his chest: an eagle placed on the heart circling a lighthouse in the center of the breastplate—the Imperial emblem used during the late Emperor Marcus II's rule.

Justinian bowed his head as the man got close. "Welcome back, Praetor."

Praetor Severus halted and examined the prisoners with his fiery green eyes. "Who are these?"

"The prisoners. They arrived early," Justinian informed him.

"Of course... Peuri's misdoings, I'd not doubt," Severus spat.

Justinian's jaws dropped. "Severus! You cannot speak about our Emperor in that way!"

The Praetor scowled at Justinian, a dark storm seeming to brew around him. Despite not moving an inch closer, nor being more than an inch taller, the Praetor seemed to loom over his Legate. "The child is across the sea, sitting on his plush throne. Are *you* going to tell him, *Justinian*?"

Justinian stared at the Praetor and just blinked. Speechless, he bowed his head.

Severus approached Yashin and inquired, "What is your name?"

Something seemed strange about the Praetor compared to the other legionaries. Could it have been a lack of disgust towards the Dwarf? The man seemed to Yashin to have less care about the Dwarf than he did Justinian.

He knelt as best as he could with his stubby legs. "Yashin Navopo, my Praetor."

"Keep grovelling, cobbler," Severus said before moving to Yashin's compatriot. "Name?"

Imbert knelt before him. "Imbert, my Praetor."

"Rise," he commanded. As Imbert stood, he moved onto the green creature. The Praetor's eyes widened, and he took in the creature's appearance. In awe the man exclaimed, "What a creature! You must be born from the womb of a mountain!"

"I am Goreg."

"As good as you would be breaking stone… I shall offer you the chance to leave this filth and join the ranks of my guard, Little Mountain. Do you vow to serve me loyally and without question?"

The massive creature shrugged. "Sure."

Severus' look of excitement turned sour, but he shrugged it off and moved onto Nurin.

The Dwarf stared uncomfortably at the Praetor, unsure of what to do. Finally Severus instructed: "Your name."

Snapping out of his trance, he fumbled out. "N-Nurin Uvazebûrzan."

"Iron-fist, correct?" Severus asked.

"Yes P-Praetor. You speak Dwarven?" Nurin asked.

"Only a little. I learned it during my command in the War of Klatvâdír Valley. In fact, I remember a Dwarven officer who called himself Ranin Uvazebûrzan."

Nurin's face turned to shock and perhaps even a little excitement. "R-Ranin was my fa-father's name. He died in that w-war."

"Must be the same Dwarf. A valiant warrior. He and his detachment held on until their last moments. We went to great lengths to capture him alive, yet I knew he would reveal nothing to us before my men even brought him to me. It saddened me to take the life of such a countryman, but 'tis war. At least Emperor Marcus had the wisdom to end that war quickly."

The Dwarf's heart visibly sank.

"Say, in honor of your late father, I shall extend to you an offer to join my guard."

"Th-thank you." The Dwarf paused for a moment before nervously finishing. "My Praetor."

"But first you must prove your allegiance to me…" Severus stated emotionlessly. His minute of kindness had overstayed its welcome. "Kiss my boot."

The Dwarf stared confused at the Praetor. Severus crossed his arms, and the Dwarf looked down at the man's boot. The Dwarf knelt down and puckered his lips. Wincing, he slowly closed in to kiss the boot. His lips grew close to the black dyed leather, only for it to be pulled away just before they touched it.

"Do not touch me with your filth!" Severus spat at the Dwarf.

Nurin ended up kissing the dirt.

Severus walked straight past Estren and onto Falnon, not even looking at her, nor giving any acknowledgement of her existence. "Name?"

"Falnon," the redhead said with a bow.

Severus nodded briefly before moving onto the last man.

This man bowed flamboyantly and spoke proudly. "Remus of the House Schneffer. I too would like to join your guard. Since the age of thirteen I trained with sword, and the spear for longer than I can recall. If you wish me to prove my prowess, I would happily spar the best fighter within your Legion."

The Praetor furrowed his brow, visibly appalled by the man's arrogance. He opened his mouth to speak, but Justinian cut him off.

"Severus, you shant bring this man into the guard. I suspect this man to have been plotting my assassination."

"Do not tell me what to do or not do, *Justinian*!" The Praetor hissed. "What have you done to address suspicion of yours?"

Justinian furrowed his brow as he struggled for an answer. After a long pause, he gave Severus a meek shrug.

The Praetor glared at his Legate and shook his head slowly. He then held an open hand out to one of his guards. "Perhaps I should let him."

The guard handed the Praetor a black sheath, a leather wrapped hilt and black enamelled pommel protruding from it. Unsheathing his *Spatha*, the Praetor instructed the man: "Kneel, Remus of House Schneffer."

The man smiled smugly as he took a knee. He threw a victorious glance at Justinian. His attention then returned to Severus with just enough time for his gloating to turn to shock as the Praetor's blade took his head off.

"Let this be an example of what becomes of troublemakers," Severus proclaimed, wiping the blood from his blade. He sheathed his Spatha and handed it back to the guard. "Justinian, these prisoners do not look tired to me. I reckon even Plenerius the Hedonist was more tired after one of his *fortnights of rest* than these miscreants appear to be now. I expect you to extract every drop of sweat and blood from their bodies. Is that understood?"

"Yes, my Praetor," Justinian obeyed.

The Praetor looked over the bay's black water and to the great galley in it. Half a dozen row boats were coming towards the shores of Mancipus. "With me I have brought more filth. Get them cutting stone from the quarry and felling trees. Without indolence. We must fortify before the next beastman attack."

*****

Yashin sat behind the counter of the Foghouse again. Several new prisoners had arrived, along with many Legionaries and numerous crates of supplies. The Imperials distributed the prisoners amongst several labour parties and sent them to do various tasks around the island. Imbert was sent to the quarry to cut stone for various construction uses. Yashin could not save him from this—he was lucky to not be sent to a labour party himself. And even if he believed he could have, Yashin needed to distance himself from the man if he was going to be of any use.

Justinian walked in the door.

"Glory to the Emperor, Yashin Navopo," Justinian greeted him.

Yashin was not going to say it. "Greetings."

Justinian took a seat on the stool in front of Yashin. "The ship has set back to the Empire. I sent your letter. If the conditions are favourable, it may arrive within the week."

"Thank you, Justinian."

The two looked at the door as it opened. Entered a middle-aged man, dressed in a beige tunic and a darker tan hooded cloak around his shoulders, with a few scrolls under his arm. But despite his common look, behind him flanked a pair of Legionaries.

"Looks like you have customers," Justinian said as he stood up. "I shall let you tend to your patronage."

"Thank you, again," Yashin told Justinian as he left the building.

The other man set the scrolls on the counter and sat on the stool beside where Justinian had been. His accompanying Legionaries did not sit, instead standing back at a distance and watching the man.

"What can I get you?" Yashin asked.

The man smiled at him, yet the Dwarf could see it was only a courtesy. "Might you have any ale?"

Yashin pulled the pitcher of ale and a cup from beneath the counter. He poured the man a drink and informed him, "That'll be ten coppers."

The man's jaw dropped. "Ten?" He looked around and to his guards, but they stood as still as statues.

Yashin pulled out a parchment and feather pen from beneath the counter. Dipping the pen in the inkpot, he asked, "Yer name?"

"Lennart Boecke?" The man told him.

On the parchment, the Dwarf recorded next to other names:

Lennart Boecke

10C

"You have two weeks to pay me. After that, I add on a copper a day."

"Ah," Lennart said. He took a sip of the ale and clapped his lips a couple times, likely in response to its rancid taste. He shook it off and took another sip before pulling a pair of round spectacles from his breast pocket and setting them in front of his squinty brown eyes.

"You don't look like an Imperial," Yashin interrupted.

"I'm not," Lennart told him.

"Then what's with the personal guard?" Yashin gestured at the Legionaries.

"I am an architect. The Empire sent me here to oversee the various construction projects here."

"So you are an Imperial?" Yashin asked.

"No, I am a man of the Free City of Illodor!" He spat, disgusted at being called an Imperial. "After Illodor fell to the Imperials, they took my family hostage and forced me to the edges of the bloody world to do their bidding." He lowered his head and clenched onto his neck-length brown hair.

"I had several businesses in Illodor. The exact fate of the city has been a mystery to me since the war started. May I ask what happened?"

"Shortly after news spread of Peuri's belligerency, we knew our city was a target of his aggressive expansion. We immediately began looking back over and updating our war plans. Being an expert in the aqueduct and irrigation systems of the city, I had drafted up plans to inundate our surrounding lands. We thought we were safe behind our walls. Some were ignorant enough to think victory was inevitable. And I was under the delusion that merely flooding them out would stop them…"

"Aye, it is shocking to hear Illodor has fallen." Surrounded by walls and towers, Illodor was renowned for being one of the wealthiest and defensive cities in the northron realms. "How long did the siege last?"

Lennart shook his head, "There was no siege. When the Legions appeared on the horizon, the Mayor and the Free Guard surrounded the Flouvern Embassy. He flew into the embassy in a mighty fit to demand answers, but he returned pale and without dignity. Then he ordered me to return home… He withdrew my inundation plans, then opened the gates for the Legion. By the time the Free Guard realised the Mayor had betrayed the city, it was too late."

"Do you believe the city would have held if it wasn't for the Mayor?"

Lennart shook his head, "I don't know. I want to say yes, but I have seen both sides now. I have seen their conquests since and have been an accomplice in many."

"In a world divided between three empires, it seems nigh possible-"

Yashin was interrupted by the door being kicked in.

A pair of Legionaries dragged one of their comrades in, his leg bent unnaturally at the thigh and a deep wound in his abdomen with slow bleeding. The man's head hung low, his skin pale and moaning weakly. Behind them followed another man, a laceration to his arm. The last man who entered was the contubernium's decanus.

The Legionaries laid the severely wounded man on the table. He moaned in discomfort and squirmed sluggishly. One soldier began putting pressure on the wound.

"Marcellus, go grab the bone lever from the castra!" The Decanus ordered.

"Aye, Decanus!" Legionary Marcellus said before he ran out of the tavern.

"Dwarf! Give us a rag," The Decanus barked.

Yashin came around the counter with an old rag in hand. Snatching it out of his hand, the Decanus began stuffing it into the wound.

Yashin sighed. "Must you really do this here?"

He gave the Dwarf a sharp look. "Yes. We do."

"Why?" Yashin questioned.

"There is not yet a valetudinarium," he answered Yashin with a hateful scowl. He then turned to Lennart, "Architect, get on it."

Lennart nodded and noted it down in a pocketbook.

Then the Decanus took off his cape. The Decanus folded it longways a few times, then placed it next to the man. With the help of his Legionary, they rolled the man over and he slid the cape under. For a minute they played with the cape, working to get it under and around the man. When the Decanus decided it was good enough, he bound it around the man's waist, putting pressure on the wound. Yashin was not sure the good it would do; the man's consciousness was slowly fading away.

Having done everything they could for that man, the Decanus moved to the other injured man, who was holding his wound. With a bit of resistance from the man, the Decanus removed his hand and looked at the wound.

"Keep holding the blood in. We will have to go to the barracks to stitch it."

The other Legionary returned to the tavern, following at the heels of the Centurion.

"What happened out there, Decanus?" The Centurion asked the Decanus.

"Centurion Ornerus! The beastman ambushed our patrol in the hills. Legionaries Kaeso, Arrius, and Curius were slain. Ju-"

"And Junus too, soon enough," Centurion Ornerus interrupted.

"We do not know that. We-"

Ornerus stopped him there. "I have seen this many times, Falx. He's too far gone. Take him back to the barracks, let him die comfortably in his bed."

"Aye, Centurion," Decanus Falx said sadly.

Falx and the other Legionary picked up the now unconscious man. Centurion Ornerus led the way out, and the Legionaries carried him out. When the tavern was empty of all but himself and Lennart, Yashin went behind the counter to grab a bucket and rag. *'What a mess they made of my tavern,'* he thought sourly.

'Who are these beastmen?' Yashin wondered as he cleaned up the blood. Perhaps that was the Imperial's new favourite word to call those they deemed "barbarians". Whomever they were, they were clearly dangerous.

◈ Chapter Five

It was again in the place Yashin spent almost all his time, the Foghouse. The stools up front were mostly taken up by Legionaries. A few more sat at the tables. After their labour shifts, the prisoners would come and drink, but they always cleared out when the Legionaries arrived a few hours later. The only prisoner that typically remained was Imbert. In his habitual spot, Imbert sat in the far, shadowy corner of the building. Wedged in the angle between two walls, he looked asleep, but Yashin knew he was awake and listening to all.

He went to a table in the middle of the room, deserted a short time ago by a group of prisoners. Setting his wooden bin on the table, he collected the mugs and set them into it. The last cup on the table was knocked over, grog spilled all over and dripping off the table. Grumpily the Dwarf threw the cup in the bin. He pulled a rag from his belt and wiped the table off, then the chair. It was then that something caught his eye. Crawling under the table, he snatched the parchment, one of its corners soaked with grog. After he emerged from under the table, he held up the heavy paper and squinted his star-field eyes to see it in the candlelight.

The Fire Wench,

Come forth all and see me, the Fire Wench. Enchantments, Charms, and Other magic needs. Listen to the whispers, find the glass of fire, or however else you may find me. Bringeth a pouch full of coins, and spare not. Come see the Fire Wench for your enchantment needs.

~ F.

When he finished reading the parchment, Yashin crumpled it up and chucked it into the bin. Letters such as these had been popping up around the colony for awhile. Nobody knew who had been posting them. He had previously suspected Remus, but he had been proved otherwise. In response, the Imperials had been on the lookout, watching everything and everyone. Yet the letters kept popping up.

And that was not the end of the colony's troubles. While the beastmen had not yet shown themselves, other than to the patrol they ambushed several weeks ago, they have been ever looming. Workers in the lumber yard and quarry repeatedly reported seeing shadows lurking in the darkness of the woods. At night one could see campfires burning, though every next day the scouts have reported them having packed up and moved. And a couple of times volleys of arrows flew from the woods and at the sentries. Yashin remained curious exactly as to what the beast men were, yet not curious enough to actually want to find out.

Going back around the counter, Yashin set the bin next to Centurion Ornerus. "More ale for any of you?"

"Aye!" Several of the Legionaries cried at once, raising their cups.

"Four coppers, boys," Yashin told them. The last ship that came through brought some rations, and he had set up a makeshift still to produce bread-wine. But it was not enough to drop prices significantly. Any day everything he needed should be arriving. That is, if his message even got through.

Performing his duty, he pulled the jug of grog from beneath the counter and began pouring cups.

"What a fool… You know he slept with the Emperor right?" Centurion Ornerus told his comrades.

"What? Tis can't be true?" Legionary Marcellus asked in shock.

"Aye it is. Everyone knows it by now," Decanus Falx told him.

"Why do you think he was sent here?" Centurion Ornerus asked. "He was the boy's lover and everybody in the Imperial court knew it. That's why the senate forced him to this hell hole."

Meanwhile Yashin finished pouring his drinks and began collecting the coin.

Legionary Marcellus could not believe what he was hearing. "Isn't he the Emperor's cousin?!"

"That's what makes it even more vile," Falx said with a look of disgust.

"Justinian to be removed already…" Centurion Ornerus grumbles.

Yashin finished counting the coins and threw them in the lockbox under the counter. Then he grabbed the bin from the counter and began to walk to the back to wash them.

Thud *Thud* *Thud*

Somebody was knocking at the door. He turned around perplexed. Nobody ever knocks on the door of the Foghouse. Walking around the counter, he set the bin down where it was previously. In the corner of his eye, he saw as Centurion Ornerus noticed the crumpled paper in the bin and pulled it out. Yashin's heart beat faster as he discretely watched the Imperial uncrumpled the paper and began reading it. Walking back around the Centurion and across towards the door, he turned his head to watch what he did. Then Ornerus quickly folded the paper and stuffed it in his pocket. Yashin quietly let out the heavy breath.

He found this odd, but he was not about to say anything about it. While he had sworn to watch and report, it was not his place to accuse a high ranking Imperial. And he thought it very likely that if the Imperial told the Praetor that he found the note in Yashin's possession—and if Yashin admitted that he had previously read the note—Yashin would be the one to pay for it.

So thus he continued towards the door.

Apprehensive yet curious, he opened the door. On the other side was a man with a receding hairline, beak nose, and brown eyes, one of which was covered by a bandage wrapped around his head. The man gave Yashin a crooked smile.

"Evening," the man said in Voron, the tongue of the western empire of Voronia.

"Borivoj," Yashin said, returning a smile. But quickly it faded into a frown. He too spoke in Voron; "What happened to your eye?"

The man called Borivoj looked down at his feet. "Krolik found me... Interrogated me..." He then looked down at his fingers, each one missing their nails, and his little finger angulated.

"Did you tell him anything?!" Yashin questioned.

"No."

"Nothing at all? If you told him anything—no matter how seemingly inconsequential—you must tell me," Yashin stressed.

"Nothing."

"You must tell me more later. Did you bring everything I requested?"

"May we come in?" Borivoj asked politely.

"Please do," Yashin told him with a grin.

Borivoj looked back out into the darkness of the night and waved. Two brute-looking men with Kinzhal swords at their hips entered the room, each one at the end of a crate. Then another two with a second crate. Following them were a pair of sailors with another crate; these were not Yashin's men.

"Through that door and down into the basement," Yashin instructed.

Then the scenery changed. A tall, skinny blonde walked in, her blonde hair almost matching in colour to her silvery dress. She had light blue eyes that gave her a nettled look, and soft pink lips that always appear pursed. Behind her was a sixteen-year-old girl, with brown hair, brown eyes, and smooth white skin. She was shorter and less skinny, though with a larger bosom to the woman before her, and a shapely buttox that her red Voron dress clung tightly to. The last girl who entered was a slightly older Elf. Of quite tainted purity, Yashin knew from the length and roundness of her ears. Despite this, she was still highly attractive with amber hair, big green eyes, and freckles on her large cheeks. Her breasts were smaller than the other two's, as most She-elve's are, but her beautiful hour-glass body in a tight and revealing cut green dress made up for it.

Following the women, one more sailor entered, carrying a much smaller crate in his arms. Yashin closed the door behind them. He then followed the parade as they went down the staircase. Nearly before the last two got through the door, he heard a horn blare outside.

AAAWOOooooo-AWOOoo

All the Legionaries in the room jumped up and made haste to the door. Imbert's eyes slowly opened, and he scrutinised every person in the room. The horn blew again.

AAWOOoooo-AAWOOOooo

"What is that?" Borivoj called up the staircase.

"I don't know yet," Yashin responded. "Set the crates where they won't be in the way and get the girls situated. I'll be back."

He shut the door behind the last sailor and waddled outside, Imbert following silently behind him.

Outside, the moonlight softly illuminated the colony. The light blue glow clashed with the harsh red light from the flames of torches as a contubernium passed the Foghouse. They held torches behind red tower shields, their shiny armour glistened with fiery reflections, and their red capes flapped as they hurried towards the walls.

Behind them waddled Nurin. He lacked the armour of a Legionary, except for a Legion's helmet on his head. Along with this, a red cape gracelessly cut for his height marked his allegiance with the guard. Clasped in his grip was a Flouvic arcuballista.

"Nurin!" Yashin called out.

The other Dwarf stopped and looked over, somewhat confused. "Yes?"

"What is happening?" Yashin asked.

"I dunno. The horns signal an attack, I suppose."

"The beastman?" Yashin asked, somewhat intrigued now.

"I would guess so," Nurin said with a shrug.

Yashin began going after the contubernium, Imbert loyally following. After a second Nurin followed. They could hear screams at the gate, and roars that sounded like something between beast and man.

Chaos. That is all Yashin could describe at the gate—which could have been better described as a hole in the wall. Torches had been thrown everywhere, flickering and waving as they were fought on top of. The Legionaries were everywhere. And amongst them were abominations. Men with the heads of bulls, or legs of goats; clawed bear's paws for hands, the long snouts of a wolf for faces; man and beast were seamlessly and randomly combined. There was no single common trait amongst them, but that they stood like men, fought with the tools of man, raged with the frenzy of beast, and screamed like demons. Beastman *was* the best word to call them, Yashin decided.

The three watched the horror, in horror.

After a minute that felt like a year, Legate Justinian and Centurion Ornerus ran by the three. Justinian was wearing his breastplate for once and had a Gladius on his belt. Ornerus was dressed in his full suit of Legionary Armor, a *pilum* in hand and a *pugio* at his hip.

"I told you we should not have wasted any time on building the gate!" Centurion Ornerus snapped.

Justinian sighed. "It would have used all the iron we have. I thought the towers would do."

His Centurion pointed at the towers on the wall, only half constructed. "The towers that aren't done yet? And that's your fault too! *You're* the one who pulled the workers."

Justinian scoffed, "Well I thought-"

The Legate stopped mid-sentence as a beastman burst from the mob and charged at them. They had the mouth, nose and ears of a cow, but angry, tormented eyes of a man. Bloodied hands flailed a rusty sword around as it charged.

MRROUOuouOURRAaahh!!!

The monster took a bolt to the chest from Nurin's arcuballista. It paused for a moment on the impact. It took a step, then another, and another. With each step it slowed. It took one final step and wobbled about before crashing to the ground, impaling itself on its own sword.

MrroUrrRrrrRr, The abomination gurgled before its eyes shut for good.

Another creature ran out. It was hairy, with a snout full of teeth, and clawed hands.

AwooOooo

A second monster followed behind it, with the head and long horns of an Ibex, and the legs to go with it.

Nurin stuck his arcuballista into the dirt and rushed to draw back the string and loading another bolt. Centurion Ornerus sent his pilum through the wolf-beast's chest as Nurin raised his crossbow. The beast tumbled to the ground, but Nurin in his panic loosed his bolt.

The second beast closed in. Imbert dove between its legs. In flight he drew the dagger hidden inside his clothes and slashed at its femoral artery. Rolling and springing onto his feet, he spun around and grabbed the creature by a horn. He pulled on the horn and fought to keep its head still as he brought his dagger up and slit its throat. Retracting his blade, he kicked the beast to the ground. He walked around the creature, always outside of grabbing distance, and watched the life drain from it.

Watching Imbert walk around the creature and to his side, Yashin noticed the silhouette of a man lurking in the alley between two buildings.

Then a burst of light blinded Yashin.

The beastmen began screaming in terror rather than rage, and the men in terror the same as they were during battle.

"The hell?!" Centurion Ornerus shouted.

Yashin squinted at the light. The torches on the ground were shooting towers of flame ten feet into the air. The shadows of beastmen ran off into the woods whence they came. Centurions too ran from the flames. To their dismay, many found they had not escaped the flames as their capes had caught flame. Frantically, they tried to rip off the infernos on their backs. Many got them off, but most had already been wounded or found their under clothes had caught fire as well. And the most unfortunate succumbed to the fiery cloaks. The torches stopped shooting flames into the air, but the flame had then engulfed the wooden palisade that surrounded the compound.

Yashin looked back to the dark alley, and the figure was long gone.

In a trance, the Centurion pulled a piece of paper out of his pocket and opened it. For a long moment, he stared at it in a woeful daze that soon turned into a mischievous look of revelation. Ornerus walked off into the night, clutching the paper in his hand.

Yashin, Nurin, Imbert, and Justinian watched as the fires burned and consumed. The roar and crackling of the flames, and the screams and moans of injured men seemed drowned out by a sort of internalised silence. The Legionaries ran past the men, crying and holding their wounds and dragging their fallen comrades. Everything was red. With blood. With fire. With burned flesh. With the colours of the Empire.

◈ Chapter Six

Finally Yashin turned and looked at the others beside him.

"Shouldn't you do something?" He asked the Legate.

Justinian's head snapped towards him with a dazed look. "Right. Men! Grab the buckets, get water from the wells or the sea. We must stop these fires!"

The men who heard him looked at him blankly. A couple were curled up into balls on the ground, others were leaning against the nearby walls breathing heavily, one was bent over throwing up, and many lay on the ground dead or dying. Justinian looked around with a twisted grimace. He began hyperventilating, and he dizzily spun around and ran off.

"What should we do?" Nurin asked Yashin.

"I am going back to my tavern. Meet me there when you are done with this mess," Yashin said. He then headed back to the Foghouse.

Imbert followed him back to the tavern. When the two entered, Yashin ordered, "Keep an eye up here."

He then proceeded down the staircase and into the basement. Beneath the Foghouse was an open foyer with chairs, tables, and a couple couches, lit by oil lamps and candles. On the back wall of the foyer was the makeshift still he erected, and the crates he had received were stacked next to it. Two pairs of rooms were to the left and right, red curtains separating each from the main room. One curtain had been left open, the She-elf sprawled out across a wide bed in nudity.

Borivoj turned to Yashin's footsteps and stood up from the couch when he saw the Dwarf. The other four quickly followed.

"What happened?" Borivoj asked in Voron.

"Chaos. Now go man the counter, Borivoj," Yashin ordered in Voron. "And get these four taking shifts guarding my tavern. And none of you will be sleeping down here!"

"Yes, master," Borivoj submitted. The five men went up the staircase and left the basement.

Yashin waddled over to the stack of crates. Set on the ground in front of the other, larger crates was the small one. He knelt down and undid the two iron latches. Then he removed a crossbow from within the box. The design was that of an ancient crossbow, not the crossbows with windlasses or draw weights that could exceed 1000lb in years to come. Alas, it was still a beautiful tool; the wood dyed black, and elegant scrollwork across the body and limbs alike. After ensuring the crossbow had not gotten damaged through its journey here, Yashin replaced the crossbow and gently shut the crate's lid.

Then he waddled over to one of the many couches and waited for Nurin. The Dwarf would come, Yashin was certain.

*****

Footsteps echoed from up the staircase and down the basement. His black, star-field eyes slowly opened. Since his curse, Yashin never truly slept. It was more so a state of deep meditation; the relaxation of his mind and body, but persistent consciousness. Nor did he need sleep in the conventional sense—he could go for days without it—but his mind and body would grow tired without it.

He turned his head to the footsteps and saw Borivoj.

"Master, a Dwarf by the name of Nurin is here to see you."

'It is about time,' Yashin thought. "Send him down."

The Voron nodded his head and went back up. He listened as the footsteps ascended, then the door opened, then as a second pair of footsteps descended, and the door shut behind him. A few moments later, Nurin was in the basement.

"What is this place?" His fellow dwarf asked in awe.

"My next venture. The prisoners must miss the touch of a woman, and the Legionaries the comfort of their wives."

Nurin looked around. The room with the drawn curtains caught his eye, and he stared at the naked She-elf for a long moment before he snapped his head away. "You built this?"

"No," Yashin told him. "It was here before we arrived."

Nurin nodded, still taking in the room. After a moment, he finally asked, "Why did you bring me here?"

"Take a seat, Nurin," Yashin gestured at a nearby couch.

The Dwarf sat down and the dark Dwarf sat across from him.

"I may not look the same as you, but we are both Kadír. Our kind must stick together."

Nurin nodded his head in thought, "Okay…"

"You may serve in their guard, but we are both their prisoners," Yashin reminded him. "They owe you nothing. They will use you for every drop of sweat and blood they can get from you, then discard you. So we must use them."

Nurin scratched at his ginger bead. "What do you want from me?"

"Do just as you were. Remain a faithful servant to the Praetor. But silently keep your true allegiance to me, your Kadír brother, and my organisation. When the opportunity arises, we together shall play our cards to not just survive, but thrive in this forsaken camp. Are you with us?"

The Dwarf furrowed his brow and moved his dark brown eyes back and forth as he thought. "Yes," he decided.

◈ Chapter Seven

The next day...

It was that time of the day again. The prisoners had gotten released from their labour parties and allowed to take part in leisure activities. Between the fresh surplus of liquor, the new "entertainment", and the arrival of fresh prisoners, the tavern was bustling with the convicts. His homely brown-haired girl was pleasuring a customer down below, the blonde was working towards her second patron of the night, and the She-elf was dancing in a customer's lap. Business was going well.

One new prisoner, a blond-haired man with chubby cheeks, was sitting at the counter and obnoxiously telling stores.

"… that be when the Senator's guards kicked the doors in and stormed the room. She was squirtin' and screamin' in so much pleasure she 'adn't even noticed. Jumped through the window still pullin' mah trousers up, and my buckle got stuck in the drapes. Got stuck half way down, mah cock dangling as the whole village looked upon 'im in awe!"

"Bull-shite!" a beefy prisoner with a shaved head shouted at the man.

"You don't know shite about my life," the man spat.

"I know your chipmunk ass ain't never fucked no senator's daughter!"

"Chipmunk? The fuck you mean chipmunk?!" The man cried, his chubby cheeks turning red.

Falnon joined in, "Ay Endyn, when your trousers were falling down as you walked in here, didn't ya tell us you believed belts to be useless?"

"I said that because my belt got me here, of course…"

"Hmm." Falnon clearly wasn't convinced.

Once again the Foghouse's door flew open, slamming as the iron handle hit the stone wall. Four legionaries enter the tavern. The two guards of Yashin's watched the Legionaries carefully, their hands resting on their swords.

"What now.?." Yashin grumbled to himself.

"Listen up filth!" Decanus Falx screamed. All eyes were on him. "The Praetor has ordered everyone to the courtyard of the Castrum. You have five minutes."

The soldiers faced about and marched out of the Foghouse. Grumbling and chairs grating filled the air as the prisoners got up and started making their way out of the tavern. The reddish last light of the day illuminated the doorway, so Yashin put on his dark tinted spectacles and began wrapping his head. When the last few prisoners exited the building, he waved to Imbert, who was still seated in the corner. The man sprung up and the two exited the tavern, leaving it under the guard of Yashin's men.

The two walked down the road, following behind prisoners dragging themselves to it and the four Legionaries marching back. The heavens bled as the clouds in the sky were crimson from the sun setting behind snow-capped mountains. On the horizon to the east, dark clouds were rolling in.

Two Legionaries stood on either side of the gate, which was wide open. A crowd of prisoners stood right after it. Yashin pushed his way through the crowd and to the front. Nobody cared to stop him, such was not an event many wanted to be at the front for. Popping out between two men, Yashin looked at what was going on in the courtyard.

To the right, three contubernium had lined up shoulder to shoulder in two rows, tower shields in one hand and spears in the other. At the other end of the block of Legionaries was Centurion Ornerus. At Yashin's end stood Nurin and Goreg, a sizable space between the two and the Legionaries. The golem smith towered next to its forge across from the Legionaries. Across the way from Yashin and past the end of the Legionaries was Praetor Severus, with Justinian standing at his right side.

Each one of the four sides stood still for a long couple minutes. After prisoners stopped joining them, Severus cleared his throat.

Severus began walking down the line of Legionaries and towards the prisoners. "I have summoned you all before me due to the unholy scourge that has plagued our camp." He stopped before the prisoners and stood with his hands clasped behind his back. "Last night, a witch cast a dark spell that turned our palisade into coal and ashes, and left many Legionaries wounded—and several dead."

The Praetor bowed his head and closed his eyes, giving a minute of silence for the fallen.

"There must be consequences for the indiscretions within this camp," Severus continued. "Firstly, I have come to realize we can no longer allow ourselves to harvest from the dark seed of magic. As such, the Golem must die!"

'BAAdrooOOn!' the Golem cried.

"Secondly, while we have not yet discovered the identity of the witch, those who have fornicated with the wielders of darkness shall be punished." Praetor Severus turned around, "Cent-"

"Hold up," the chipmunk faced man, Endyn, interrupted. The man stood two down from Yashin, next to Falnon, whom was looking quite pale.

The Praetor stopped immediately and spun around, his face glaring with anger.

"Who are you to be orderin' us around?" Endyn questioned.

The Praetor got in the man's face, the dark storm brewing again. "I am Severus Claudus, the Praetor of Mancipus."

The man's demeanour remained foolishly bold. "Well, what crime did you commit to get sent here?"

"I'm a *murderer*," Severus hissed. Endyn only seemed to notice the Praetor's knife after it was driven into the soft tissue of his abdomen and slipped up behind his rib cage. Severus withdrew his blade as quickly as he had drawn it. Endyn looked down and held his guts in horror.

The prisoners and Legionaries alike stood in shock and horror, Justinian most of all.

"Have you lost your mind, Severus?!" The Legate gasped.

Severus approached his Legate, cleaning his knife as he walked. "I will not be questioned. Especially not by filth such as yourself." The Praetor stopped in front of Justinian and, without taking his eyes off the Legate, ordered; "Centurion Ornerus, grab the *evidence*."

"Yes, my Praetor," the Centurion said, trying to hide a smirk. He planted his tower shield firmly in the dirt and leaned his pilum against it, then went inside the tower behind him. A few moments later, he returned, holding a sheathed gladius. He handed it to the Praetor, then returned to his gear.

The Praetor kept the sword in its sheath and held it for Justinian to see. "Do you recognize this, Justinian?"

The Legate dug in his lengthy blonde hair and scratched his scalp. "A Gladius?"

The Praetor unbuckled the sheath and drew the sword. As it came free from the sheath, fire ran from the guard and down the length of the blade. He then held it high in the air, fire consuming and swirling around the blade.

Justinian's eyes widened in woe.

"Are you going to confess *now*?" Severus demanded.

Justinian furrowed his brow. "Confess to what-now?"

"We found it under your bed," Ornerus told him with a toothy grin.

"What? It isn't mine!" Justinian cried.

"Oh, is it not? How did it get under your bed then?" The Praetor questioned.

Justinian looked around and at everyone, "It must've been there from before we were assigned here!"

Severus shook his head, "What a poor excuse, Justinian."

Yashin did not think the Legate was lying. In fact, he believed he knew the identity of who placed the sword under his bed. Despite this, he was not going to interrupt…

Justinian's look of shock and helplessness turned to frustration. "It's *not* mine! And what so if it were? Emperor Peuri has decreed leeway on the use of magic in times of war!"

"May Emperor Peuri be damned to hell's fires! Our Church has not. Emperor Marcus did not. The boy emperor has betrayed everything his father stood for. Worse even; he has betrayed the Empire on every front! I shall restore our Empire starting with yourself."

"That's it, Servus," Justinian said. Then he drew his sword.

Severus spun the flaming sword in his hand so the tip was facing down. He threw the sword down, its tip digging into the earth and sticking out of the ground still aflame. Drawing his Spatha, he said, "Are you saying you are going to fight?"

"I am going to kill you, Severus," Justinian snarled. Never taking his eyes off Severus, he called to the Legionaries: "Join me now. If you do not at this very moment, you shall be deemed the enemy as well."

For a long moment, all stood still. Nobody dared move, not even the prisoners. Finally a Legionary stepped forth and crossed onto Justinian's side. Then another. And another. When all settled in on their sides, the Legionaries had divided themselves near in half.

"Badroon, let none interfere as I handle Severus," Justinian ordered the golem.

'BaaaaDROOON,' it rumbled, glaring at the Praetor. The Golem stepped in the middle to separate the two rival leaders from all others.

"What do you think you're doing, Justinian?" Severus questioned.

"I am going to replace you as Praetor of Mancipus," Justinian proclaimed. Then he charged Severus and swung his sword at the Praetor's head.

The Praetor raised his sword and blocked the blow with ease.

As all eyes were on the duel that had begun, Centurion Ornerus raised his pilum. "Traitors!" He screamed as he sent the pilum into one rebel's face.

Severus returned the strike with two quick slashes of his own. Justinian managed to parry them both, the second one almost catching him off guard.

The two opposing Legions remained inactive, befogged by the chaos. Centurion Ornerus drew his pugio and charged, and the loyalist Legionaries followed his lead. The two Legions crashed into one another. A few spears hit their foes, others got stuck in their shields, and others were abandoned after they missed. The men began drawing their Gladiuses and pushing their shields against each other.

Yashin's fellow prisoners fled the carnage in the courtyard. Nurin appeared dazed and stumbled back from the fighting. George mused over the conflict from where he towered from the beginning. Eventually the giant's expression turned to frustration and he turned to Yashin for guidance. And Yashin, not letting excitement overtake him, took his time to assess the situation. Now was not the time to run, lest the outcome be against his favour. But which outcome was in his favour? Was he to stay loyal to the Praetor or support Justinian's coup?

He then turned to Imbert, who was patiently waiting for his queue. "Run to the Foghouse and fetch my crossbow!"

The two leaders continued to spar, each one deflecting the other's blows. Severus took a step back, disengaging from combat. Severus spoke in their parley.

"Are you actually such a fool to think you will just be allowed to become the Praetor by killing me? The Empire may have descended into chaos under Peuri's rule, but we are not that savage yet!"

"The Emperor is across the sea. Who's going to tell him? It won't be you, Severus," Justinian snarled. His eyes were full of rage and a slight smile showed his enjoyment to finally be letting it all out. He lunged forward and thrust his blade.

Severus stepped out of the way and brought his own sword up. He swung it at Justinian's face, the rebel barely stumbling back in time to dodge it.

Bringing his blade up, Justinian parried another one of Severus' blows.

As the two continued sparring, Yashin started forward. "Come Nurin," he called as he went behind the Legions that were still clustered together like warring ant hills.

The Dwarf waddled after the tavernkeep, crossbow in hand. Goreg followed behind him, seemingly confused by the mutiny. In his hands was a great two-handed battle axe.

From the other side, Badroon watched the approaching non-humans. When they began nearing too close, he stepped in front of him.

The three paused, but after a moment Yashin tested his ground. After only getting one step in, the golem lunged forward and flexed its arms.

'BAaaAdroOon'

The Dwarf paused, his glare at the thing blocking his path hidden beneath his mask. "Nurin, aim for the core."

Nurin looked at Yashin as if he was crazy. "What?!"

"Do it!" Yashin barked. He knew a little about golems, having had one guarding his vault before his adversary killed it. It did not take much force to cause the crystaline core to crack, from which a great eruption of energy would occur.

Nurin raised his crossbow apprehensively and fired at the glowing crystal core between the holes of its trunk.

'baaaDROOOON!'

The golem rumbled loud enough that Yashin could feel the vibrations under his feet. Badroon began running at the men, shielding his fragile core with his trunk like arms.

Suddenly Centurion Ornerus jumped infront of the golem with his tower shield. He planted the shield in the ground and braced his body against it. The golem hit him with all its weight, yet he stood firm. Ornerus was pushed at least five feet back before the golem stopped, the dirt from under his feet in a huge pile behind him.

Badroon took a step back, and the three non-humans took two steps back themselves. Ornerus slowly backed up to the non-humans, never taking his eyes off the monster. Nurin held his crossbow only slightly lower than he had shot at. Seeing such, Yashin extended his short arm and pushed Nurin's aim towards the dirt.

Severus took two steps back and held his sword pointed at Justinian. The Praetor stood tall and had not yet broken a sweat.

The rebel let his opponent break. His face was flushed, his brow was furrowed, and his breaths had grown heavy.

Again the Praetor spoke in parlay; "Don't you think the Senate will wonder what happened to their Praetor? Or the half of the Legionaries stationed here that are now missing? What delusions you do have if you believe your coup will go unnoticed…"

"The Emperor will protect me," Justinian said between breaths.

"The Emperor will *crucify you*, Justinian," Severus hissed. "What madness drives you to be so blindly loyal to the boy, anyways?"

"I-" Justinian cut himself off. He struggled finding the words he wished to use. After a moment he shook his head in frustration. "I love him! First auntie when he was wee, and now Marcus too, I've been the only one there for him."

Severus' eyes slightly turned away from Justinian and off into nowhere. Then he began slowly nodding his head. "Ah, so *you're* the reason Peuri is the way he is. Everything makes sense now."

Justinian's mouth opened slightly and his sword dropped about as much. "What does that mean?!"

"The boy is a fool. He has stretched the Legions too thin, broke the Empire's economy, plunged us into sin, created too many enemies within his own court…" Severus stopped himself from listing the Emperor's faults endlessly.

"That is why I should be there to guide him and protect him, not stuck on this god-forsaken island!" The rebel proclaimed.

A sinister grin formed across Severus' face. "Do you know who you need be protecting him from?"

Justinian went into deep thought. His sword drooped a little farther. For what felt like an eternity, he thought.

Severus finally gave up waiting for an answer. "Oh Justinian, what a failure you are. For a minute you led me to question whether I had underestimated you. Now I know definitively that you are unfit to replace me." There was a sort of calmness in his voice, yielding feelings of disappointment. But could also hear his disgust. "Just drop this bloody coup…"

Justinian looked down at his sword, it drooping low and unguarded. Slowly he uncurled his fingers until it slid out of his hand and at his feet. He stared at the sword he gave to the dirt as he whimpered; "Enough…"

It was about this time that Imbert returned, crossbow and quiver in hand, and Yashin's four thugs at his side. Quickly Yashin took the crossbow and loaded a bolt.

"Ya here that?" Ornerus shouted at the remaining living Legionaries. Slowly they stopped pushing and stabbing. The rebels too gave their weapons to the dirt and went to their knees, and the loyalists put blades to the rebel's throats.

Badroon's tense posture relaxed some as he looked to the demoralised Justinian. Realising the fight was over, Badroon sulked back over to his forge.

"Take them to the dungeons!" Ornerus shouted. As his Legionaries marched their prisoners away, he grabbed a spear from the ground and went up to Justinian. The man did not look at him. All the former Legate did was stare at the ground. Ornerus stabbed Justinian with enough force to cause some pain but not truly do him harm, and the broken man began walking.

As Ornerus began to take Justinian to the dungeon, Yashin approached the Praetor who stood watching, followed by his men. And Goreg, his axe still unbloodied.

"My Praetor, I have information I believe I should relay to you," Yashin told him.

Severus looked to the Dwarf. "What is it?"

"I have reason to believe Centurion Ornerus planted the magic sword, to cause turmoil in your ranks and seize power for himself."

"You best not be attempting to save Justinian, are you Dwarf?" The Praetor warned.

Yashin shook his head. "Justinian is a traitor. But so is Ornerus."

Severus gave the Dwarf a nod in understanding. "Centurion Ornerus!"

Ornerus waited with Justinian outside the door to the dungeon, the Legionaries before him bottlenecked at it. He looked to the Praetor.

"Come here."

"Yes, my Praetor," Ornerus said. He proceeded to tap Justinian with the head of his spear and barked, "Come!"

"Leave him there," Severus ordered.

Turning his spear up towards the air, the man froze in confusion. Justinian for the first time looked up. Ornerus looked back to Justinian before walking towards the Praetor.

A good distance away, the Praetor barked, "There's good enough!"

The Imperial complied, his face plastered with confusion.

"Were you whom put the cursed sword under Justinian's bed?" The Praetor questioned. His Centurion opened his mouth, but before the man got any words out, Severus added: "Don't lie to me."

Ornerus was silent for a moment before admitting, "I did."

"So you sought to undermine my regime."

"I only wished for the removal of Justinian. He was unfit to be this camp's Legate," Ornerus told the Praetor. He stood tall and spoke loud, but Yashin could hear the man's nerves through the cracks.

"Justinian was part of this regime, and your superior. Clearly you lack respect and honour."

Ornerus opened his mouth to refute, but before he could get any words out Severus ordered Yashin, "Execute him."

"Yes, Praetor," Yashin complied. "Nurin?"

Nurin loaded a bolt onto his crossbow.

"No! I was helping you, my Praetor! You must understand—you must!" Ornerus pled, his strong demeanour dissolving into panic.

Yashin aimed at the Ornerus' chest and let a bolt fly. It went deep into Ornerus' shoulder and his face lit up in pain. Then came Nurin's, first piercing the man's breastplate then his heart. Ornerus fell to his knees, tears in his eyes. Yashin loaded another bolt and sent it into the middle of his chest. The Centurion gazed blankly at the bolts in his body and fell to his knees. For what felt like an eternity as the Dwarves reloaded their crossbows, the man stared at the bolts and wobbled on his knees. Nurin sent the last bolt into his eye. His body finally wedded the dirt, their eternal matrimony consummated with his blood.

Justinian, tired and defeated, glanced upon the scene with disinterest before gazing into nothingness.

Yashin knew the Praetor would not bestow such mercy upon Justinian.

◈ Chapter Eight

Two sentries stood posted on the great wall of black, charred wood. From end to end of the wall, shore to shadowy shore of the small peninsula, the palisade was burned. And like the wall, the relationship of the two sentries was equally burned. One Legionary was a loyalist, and the other a rebel. This is the way it had been since they had been released a couple days ago; the rebels under constant scrutiny. The once undying trust and camaraderie that once existed in the Imperial Legions was now shattered.

From the treeline, which had been cut back far from the compound, the sentries could see a bush rustling. The men squinted and watched apprehensively. Soon a figure emerged, still obscured in the shadowy treeline. The men drew their swords and looked at each other in the corner of their eyes, wondering if the other was going to stage their death as a casualty of the coming beastmen attack.

But it was not a beastman who emerged, instead it was a normal—though tattered—man. His beard reached down past his navel, which was exposed beneath his torn rags. He stumbled towards the guards, tired and weak.

One Legionary raised his horn and blasted it once.
Aaa-WOOOOoo

*****

Yashin sat in the empty Foghouse. It was always empty this time of the day, but business had been hurting even in the other parts of the day. Between the beastmen attacks and the coup, the number of Legionaries was dwindling. As a result of fewer guards, and likely Severus' mistrust that the rebels may recruit them for a second coup, there had been new restrictions placed on when and how the prisoners could spend their free time. Even so, all he had to pay for was the liquor and his workers. Not only did he own the tavern free of charge, the empire even transported all his supplies for free. He was making an easy profit, and he was far from his enemies—other than Severus, whom he actually felt safer under than the rest of the Flouvern itself.

Aaa-WOOOOoo

The sound of the horn blew. He waited for another, but it never came. Jumping down from the bar stool, he waddled towards the door. Then he waved one of his guards to follow him. They stood out of the tavern, the sun coming close to its zenith. Looking around there was nothing. Then two Legionaries came around a building, carrying a man between the two of them.

His greasy black hair was long and tangled, as was his beard. The clothes on his back seemed to be on the brink of turning to dust. The man clearly was not Legionary, and Yashin did not recognize him as a prisoner.

A contubernium marched from the Castrum and met the two Legionaries. They had the two with the man take the lead and marched back to the Castrum. Yashin waddled behind them, accompanied by his guard.

They took the man up the road and to the Castrum. Through the courtyard they passed, then into the grand hall. Yashin waddled behind without any question. At the center of the hall within the colonnade was Severus, sitting in his Curule. The Legionaries gathered around Severus. Before his authority, they let go of the man and he fell to his knees. Yashin, and in suit his guard, stayed at the back of the hall.

"Who is this?" Severus questioned.

The man mumbled in a foreign language that Yashin did not understand.

"A Kraft!" The Legionary announced. "He walked up to our camp."

"Has he said anything?" Severus asked.

"Not that we could understand, Praetor."

"Send in the translator," Severus ordered the Centurion. "And not all of you need be here."

"Aye Praetor!" The Centurion obeyed. He then marched out, taking his contubernium with him, leaving just the two Legionaries who carried the man in, Yashin, and the bodyguard.

They stood in silence for a minute, the man twitching and looking blankly as he took in the grand hall. The silence was broken by the sound of a door unlatching. As the door creaked open, a loud methodical whooshing sound came from behind. A creature with red skin bobbed into the room, staying at about a foot above the floor. It was about three feet in height and looked somewhat humanoid, but for several differences; its ears were like that of a bat's; where a man's hair should be was replaced by two large goat-like horns; its feet had two large tows and a dewclaw, and its hands two fingers and a thumb; its body was covered in long, thick hairs akin to that of a horse's eyelashes; and it had a long fork-tail. Two small, yellow eyes with reptilian pupils flanked either side of its flat, stubby nose. Yashin was familiar with the species; it was an Imp.

Bobbing into the middle of the colonnade, the Imp landed a respectful distance from the Praetor and pulled its wings in tight. It lowered its head before speaking; "You requested my presence, master?"

"Do you speak Kraft, Imp?" Severus asked it.

"Yes master." Its words revealed its pointy, doglike teeth. "I can fluently speak Flouvic, Flavian, Kraft, and Voron. I am also familiar with various regional dialects."

"Enough. Ask this man who he is." Severus ordered.

"Yes master," it recited. Looking at the man, its raspy voice spoke in the same foreign language that Yashin knew was Kraft.

"Adelmar Hilgersohn," the man responded to the Imp.

The Imp began telling the Praetor, "Adelmar, son of-"

"Yes, I understood that," Severus interrupted. "I am asking you to find out what he is doing in Mancipus."

The Imp translated the question into Kraft, and the man spent his time replying to the Imp.

When the man finished speaking, the Imp translated to the Praetor; "He was a sailor aboard a merchant vessel. A storm swept his vessel away from shore and left his ship stranded on the island many moons ago."

Severus furrowed his brow. "Where is the rest of his crew?"

Again, the Imp translated and diligently listened to the man's response.

"The man says his ship washed up next to a strange vault, of sorts, in a mountainside. As a storm battered them for days, they spent all their time trying combinations in some kind of magic sundial. After they managed to open the vault, he refused to enter the vault. He says he felt something evil inside. While he was waiting outside, he heard the screams of his shipmates. And something evil. He ran in fear, and from that point on he had been hunted by what we call the beastmen."

Severus looked fascinated. "Can he tell us where this vault is?"

Once again the Imp asked and the man responded.

"Yes."

"And the combination?"

The Imp repeated the process.

"He believes so."

"Take the man to get cleaned and rested," Severus ordered the Legionaries. "You may leave, Imp."

"Yes master," the Imp complied. He stretched out his wings and began flapping them. With great gusts of air, he lifted up about a foot and bobbed back out of the room.

Yashin turned and took a step towards the door, but he was stopped when Severus spoke.

"Dwarf!"

The barkeep turned around nervously. "Yes, Praetor?"

"Before his betrayal, Justinian told me of the… deal you made with him. It was wise of you to not take his side."

"I made a deal to assist the Empire, not Justinian. He was merely the representative of the Empire whom I made it with."

Severus nodded his head. "Wise. To continue your little deal, I have a task I bestow upon you."

"Yes?"

"I am going to send an expedition to this vault, and you are going to lead it. You will take Justinian with you."

"Yes, Pr-" Yashin began.

"I am not finished. See to it that he does not return. Ever. A few of my Legionaries will accompany you along your mission. You may take whomever of the prisoners you see fit, as well."

Yashin nodded his head.

"You may leave now," the Praetor ordered. "Be prepared to leave when the sun rises."

Yashin turned around and started towards the door.

"Oh, and take the Golem," Severus commanded after him.

*****

Darkness surrounded him. The light emitted from his lantern was only enough to see the step in front of him. His footsteps echoed as he descended the staircase down into the bowels of the Castrum. The slight flickers of light on the walls around him disappeared to absolute darkness, and the floor levelled out below him. He turned to his left and walked forward until the lantern nearly crashed into wrought-iron bars. Squinting into the darkness, he could see naught past them. He squeezed the lantern between the bars and lit up the cell as much as he could. Inside was a pair of young men chained to the wall, their heads and cheeks were overgrown, and their pants were soiled. The putrid smell of decay and faeces burned at Yashin's nostrils.

He wiggled the lantern back through the bars and walked down to the next set of bars. Again he stuck the lantern through. Inside was a beastman chained by the arms and legs. Its ears flicked up at the clanking sound of the lantern. Slowly its eyes opened and it snorted with its bovine nose. The creature stood up and charged towards Yashin. The Dwarf did not flinch, as he already knew that it was going to be stopped dead in its tracks. Violently halted, the creature swayed back and forth before collapsing to the ground.

Yashin continued down the line. Sticking the lantern into the third cell he found the creature he was looking for. Justinian sat in the corner, his knees pulled up to his chest and his face buried into his palms. Yashin raised his other hand and put a key into the door. The lock clicked loudly as he turned the key. The door creaked loudly as it swung open and he took a step in.

Not looking up from his palms, Justinian said, "Is it finally time for me to die?"

"No," Yashin said.

Justinian looked up, his eyes filled with rage. His once well kept beard had grown a couple inches, and had become tangled and greasy. "*You*," he hissed.

"Aye, tis I."

Justinian stood up and took the single step at Yashin that he could before the chain around his foot caught. "You betrayed me!"

"No, I fulfilled my end of the bargain. My services provided to the Empire in return for leniency, not to serve you, don't you remember?"

"Stop spouting bullshite, we both know you chose the side you bet would win. That's what you do, isn't it? Anything to improve your situation, regardless of how immoral it may be."

Yashin chuckled and peeled his lips back. "I think I made the winning bet. Wouldn't you agree?"

Justinian glared at Yashin for a long moment. Then Yashin threw the key at his feet. The man looked down at the keys perplexed, then looked suspiciously at the Dwarf.

"The Praetor decided you are not worth feeding or watering if you aren't going to work for it like everybody else."

Justinian smiled and laughed as he bent down to grab the key, "So the slaver becomes the slave… Where's he putting me, the quarry?"

Yashin shook his head. "No. He is sending us to some temple on the other side of the island."

"*Us?*" He asked as he undid his shackles.

"You and myself; several of the prisoners; a handful of your comrades. And the Golem."

"When do we go?" Justinian asked, rubbing his wrists where the shackles had resided for weeks on end.

"As soon as you get that chain off your leg."

"What time is it out there..?"

"Sun just rose a little ago," Yashin answered.

His ankle freed, Justinian tossed the key back at Yashin. The dwarf stuffed it in his pocket; he might need it later. With the lantern he leads Justinian back through the blackness and up the stairs. Slowly they ascended, Justinian just a step behind him. When they reached the door, Yashin threw it open. He passed through, but when he turned to close it he saw Justinian still standing there. The man was covering his eyes with his hands. Slowly he removed them and opened his eyes just a slit. He squinted in pain, trying to get his bearings of the outside world again. Justinian had not seen the sun since his mutiny, Yashin knew.

"Come on, get out," Yashin ordered the former Legate.

Justinian stepped out of the stairway and into the courtyard. Around the two were now Imbert, Nurin Ironfist, Falnon, and one contubernium of Legionaries.

The Decanus approached the two. "Are you done yet, Dwarf?"

"No," Yashin stated bluntly.

The Decanus furrowed his brows. "No?"

"This man does not have a weapon."

"A weapon? The traitor cannot be-"

"My good *Dekarchos*, what may be the point of bringing him along if we are not going to use him? Just for him to watch us get killed? To suck your cocks?"

Several Legionaries struggled to restrain themselves. One in particular leaned in to his comrade and whispered heedlessly: "If we were thirteen year old boys, Justinian would enjoy that wouldn't he?"

Paying no heed to their comments, Yashin went on. "Pardon me, *Dekarchos*, I did not mean to speak out of place. I just do not wish upon you Severus' wrath for making such a miscalculation."

The Decanus murmured to himself as he turned to the armoury. He looked back over his shoulder to glare at the Dwarf.

"Got that cocky have you, Dwarf? Being Severus' puppet will only protect you so long," Justinian said, a hint of joy briefly reappearing at the implication of Yashin's demise.

"In all likelihood, at least one of us will be too dead to care after this."

Justinian shrugged.

The Decanus stormed back to the two, a Gladius in hand. He shoved the flat side against Justinian's stomach and spit, "If you're going to turn this on any of us, traitor, kindly make it the Dwarf first."

Yashin   chuckled   at   the   comment.

◈ Chapter Nine

A light sprinkling came down from above, and dark ominous clouds were rolling in on the horizon. This did not bother Yashin, for he was concealed from the world with tightly woven fabrics. His legs had grown sore from days of walking. This also did not bother him, for he had walked a great many steps in his enumerated days in this world. The men grew increasingly bitter with every step they took. Their bodies ached and they all had enough of one another before they even started their mission. If the others had not hated him before, they did now. It was Yashin they blamed for being here, as if it was by his will that they were here and not the Praetor's. He wondered what Imbert's opinion of all this was, as the boy was as cryptic and emotionless as the Golem they had dragged with them. But did what the others think bother him? No, he has been hated by men since the day he entered this world.

It did bother him that they had not yet found this vault yet, however.

They had been travelling for days, following the coastline except for when they could not for one reason or another. It could be back in any of the sections they went around. Even now they diverted around a steep mountain, and it could be along the shore back on the other side of the mountain. He had no clue how large this isle was, and he did not want to find himself back at the camp, especially with Justinian still alive. If they found themselves attacked by the beastmen, perhaps he could slay the man in the chaos, yet they had managed to avoid the beastmen all this time. One night they heard their drums and roars in the near distance, but a fire broke out between the two camps while Falnon was out relieving himself. For two days acres of forest burned behind them. And even with his need to kill Justinian, a beastman attack was not something Yashin hoped to happen. And it was unlikely they would continue to evade them if the mission continued much longer.

Luckily, it would not.

As they reached the crest of the sloping hill they were climbing to avoid the much taller mountain, they looked out into the small valley between another mountain and the one they were travelling around. Beached on the tall rocks of the gravelly shore was a merchant galley. Its sails were torn and disintegrating, and debris was scattered across the beach.

"Could this be?" Justinian asked.

"Look there!" The Decanus exclaimed.

"Where?" Yashin asked.

"There," Nurin told Yashin as he pointed at the adjacent mountainside.

Knowing where to look, Yashin made out what was likely a series of stairs wider than they were long going up the mountainside, all leading to what Yashin could make out as a portico extending out from the steep mountainside.

"Well are we going to stand in the rain or get to it?" Yashin asked before he started down the hill.

'Badroon,' the golem creaked.

The others started following.

Previously every step felt like it took a year to take, but now with a goal in their eyes, every ten steps felt like just one. In what felt like only a few minutes they were to the stream that flowed down the valley. With their newfound surge of energy, they quickly used the rocks and boulders resting in its drowsy current. Yashin carefully found a way across despite his stubby legs, yet when he turned around his fellow dwarf Nurin was looking dumbfounded at the water.

'Baaaaadroon,' the golem creaked sadly. It then picked up the dwarf by the collar, splashed straight across the stream, and gently returned the Dwarf to the earth.

Yashin turned back and he found the men were already a great distance away, none having not stopped for the dwarves—none but Imbert.

The three chased the others across the rest of the clearing. The sounds of waves crashing on the nearby beach were the only sounds to be heard, for if there were any others they were too faint against them. Yashin could see the ocean winds blowing in Imberts unkempt hair, and Nurin shivering as it sucked the heat out of him; the dark dwarf could feel nothing, he could only observe. Carrying on with his two compatriots made him for a moment happy--gave him the feeling of having friends. But it lasted for only a moment, as he quickly corrected himself. Imbert could never be trusted and Nurin was a fool. Both were just assets to be used for his ends.

Quickly they made it to the other side of the valley. Stone stairs ascended up the steep slope of the mountain, and at the top rested the portico. The men ahead of Yashin stopped at its base when they finally looked back for the Dwarves. Yet in their excitement they decided they could not wait a moment for the Dwarves and rushed the grand staircase. Yashin stopped before the first step, his sigh muffled by his mask. Nurin was happy to stop along with him, already fatigued from the days of travelling, and Imbert waited first for Yashin like a loyal dog. The golem that had been mechanically trailing behind them passed the trio without hesitation and ascended the stairway two steps at a time.

Yashin took the initiative, as his two compatriots clearly were not going to. Taking the first step he already knew the ascent was going to be an ordeal. Most steps built for humans are hard enough, and these were taller yet. But he took the next. And the next.

After five steps he turned back. He saw Nurin on the first step struggle to the second. Then the poor dwarf merely stared at the third in agony. Imbert stood just behind him, watching the Dwarf with a sad look.

"Come on Nurin!" Yashin exclaimed.

"I..." Nurin could hardly find the time to speak between his bellowing breaths. "Can't..."

"Yes you can! I am just as tall as you, and I'm doing it."

"My legs... I used to track game for days, but now... Too much time in camp." Nurin admitted in an airy voice, his head drooped in shame.

"Then it is time to get your legs strong again!" Yashin lectured in woefully forced cheerfulness.

"They have turned to aspic jelly!" the Dwarf whined.

"Just take the next step. One step." Yashin told him.

Nurin whimpered as he began climbing his little body up the step. When he finally made it up he stopped and bent over in exhaustion.

"Okay, now another," the dark dwarf encouraged, and Nurin repeated.

"Another!" He repeated. Then another time for his compatriot to be on the same step. Then he placed his hand on Nurin's shoulder, "Now just follow me."

Then he took off. Nurin followed for several more steps until they were about a third of the way up before stopping again, and it wasn't until Yashin was half way up that he took notice.

"See how easy that was, you're almost there."

"I can't... Just let me rest for a little," Nurin pleaded.

"You can rest at the top. The others are waiting on us."

Nurin nodded his head and began taking more steps. Yashin waited until Nurin was just a couple steps below him to continue himself. About another third of the way up, Yashin heard Imbert say behind him, "Keep going my friend." Just as Yashin turned around, the Dwarf nodded and began up the steps again.

Finally Yashin made it to the top.

"What took you so long?" The Decanus snarled at Yashin.

"One in our party was in need of motivation. Unfortunately, Decanus, there are those in this world who were not blessed with strong will. Or long legs."

The Decanus furrowed his brow and glared at the Dwarf momentarily before turning away. The Imperial must have been unsure of what to make of his comment, Yashin thought. "Here is the door the Kraft spoke of. And is the sundial apparatus."

Placed directly in the centre of the portico was a hulking, spool shaped table of stone vaguely reminiscent of a giant garden sundial. Twenty stone keys spiralled out from the centre of the table, each bearing its own unique foreign character inlaid with a strange glassy stone. Parallel to the table was a large vault door embedded into the stoney face of the wall that had been cut from the mountain.

The Decanus procured a folded parchment from his tunic's pocket and fumbled to unfold it for study. "Fuckin' shite..." he mumbled before extending his hand out to the table and resting his calloused fingers on one of the keys. Everybody held their breath as he depressed the key with a grinding stone sound. Suddenly the key made a snappy click and the Decanus recoiled his hand apprehensively. The key remained depressed within the table, and a fiery light lit ever so faintly within the glassy stone. A moment passed before the Decanus looked down again at the parchment and studied it. He repeated the process with the next key, then the next, each time getting a little faster until he had recessed five of the twenty keys. Nothing happened. Uneasily he looked back and forth between the parchment, the table, and the door. Everybody else was watching him.

"Well that's what the damned drawing said..." he spat.

"Are you sure you put it in right?" One of his Legionaries asked.

"I don't know," he growled in frustration. "The drawing is all wrong! There's seventeen keys on this paper and twenty on the sundial."

"One should trust a Kraft as much as they should a Dwarf..." Justinian muttered in his sulking away from everyone else.

"Maybe it's six keys not five?" Falnon pitched in.

"‚Damn hope not!" The Decanus exclaimed. He quickly attempted forcing down a sixth key, but it would not budge. He sighed in relief, "Nay, appears not.."

"What now?" A Legionary asked.

"Can we not put in another?" Another asked.

"The sailor claimed they tried combinations for two days," Yashin explained. "They must have done something to reset it. I find it highly doubtful that it just so happened to break when we found it."

"And might you have any theories on how to do that, huh Dwarf?" the Decanus questioned.

"Mayhaps you should try the centre stone? It is the only one that is completely round rather than a sector."

Visibly uncertain of whether it would work, the human pushed the round center key in. A loud chorus of clicks rang out as all the keys very slowly returned to their starting positions, the dim lights snuffed out in the blink of an eye.

"Lets try this again." The Decanus inputted the combination as he had before, but changed one key to the one next to it. Nothing happened. He reset it and put in another, again only changed by one key, and nothing happened.

"Oi, let me do it!" One of his Legionaries tried pushing him out of the way.

The Decanus pushed him back. "Nay! I can figure it out!"

He started inputting another combination, but midway through the Legionary leant over and started pressing a couple of the keys in.

"Curse you!" The Decanus spat.

While everybody else's eyes were on the two arguing men, Yashin was having a look around. Laying around the portico were crates of supplies, many of which were cracked open, rotting away or being picked at by the wildlife; bedrolls and blankets shimmied anywhere at all protected from the elements; and numerous personal items scattered about. But only one thing seemed to be of any interest to Yashin: a leatherbound book cast to the ground.

The Dwarf waddled over to it and reached down for it. He cracked open the book and flipped to the last entry. Nobody could see the triumphant smile behind his mask. The only person who paid any attention to the Dwarf rather than the Imperials fighting over the combination was Justinian. When Yashin tried to make eye contact, the former Legate's eyes snapped away back to staring at nothing.

Book in hand, Yashin pushed his way in between the fighting Imperials.

"Enough," he commanded. He entered his own combination reminiscent of the one drawn for them, but not what Yashin would have considered to be very close.

A loud crash and a thud startled the men. Then all went silent for just a moment followed by a terrible rumbling and roaring. The rounded vault door rolled itself open, retreating within the stoney walls, before slamming to a halt.

Yashin set the book upon the table, opened to the page illustrating the correct combination as recorded by the ship's Yeoman.

"Who shall go first?"

"Traitor, you're up!" The Decanus barked.

Justinian shuffled from the spot he was cowering at and into the vault. The contubernium went in behind him, pushing him along.

The man Falnon took a couple steps towards the door before suddenly stopping. Furrowing his brow, he asked, "Should they not be sending us ahead of them? Is that not what we are here for?"

"Shhh! Don't give them any ideas!" Nurin shrieked.

"They are simple soldiers, my friend. They put their own glory before logic," Yashin told him.

Yashin strutted into the vault, tailed by the other prisoners. It was shadowy within the mysterious structure. The Legionaries wrapped torches with rags while the Decanus stood guard over them, particularly keen on the traitor.

"Damn it is bitter cold in here…" One whined. Yet Yashin was well insulated beneath all the layers of shielding from the sun. In fact, Yashin preferred the cold even without the warming clothes, his Dwarven people hailing from crisp mountain peaks. This was one of many reasons Yashin would never visit the Soutron realms. That along with knowledge that the nonhumans fare even worse under rule of the Southrons than the Northrons—before the reign of Peuri, at least.

One of the Legionaries produced a wineskin and doused the others' torches with its contents, and its foul odor penetrated Yashin's mask many times stronger than the cold. As he did that, another produced a band of steel and wore it around his nuckles. He struck a flint across it and sent sparks raining down upon his torch that lay on the stone floor. He struck twice and thrice, and when for a moment it appeared to need fourth striking, it burst into flames. Raising the torch back in the air, the fire was passed along to another torch, then passed onto the next, and passed forth until all torches were lit, long tongues of fire frantically licking the air in the draft. In the harsh, flickering light Yashin took in his surroundings. Inside the was a long tunnel with arches bracing the flat ceiling, square wooden doors cut into the walls, and a staircase descending further into the depths. Looking back towards the vault door, Yashin noticed a round protrusion in the wall.

"Enough with your time wasting, men!" The Decanus opened. "Start searching the place."

Swords and spears in hand, the Legionaries began kicking in the wood doors. Nobody—besides Imbert, whom he barely regarded as anything more than his second shadow anymore—paid any mind to Yashin as he headed back to the entrance and examined the strange protrusion. It matched the round centerstone of the dial outside, except this one was cracked and crushed in, the crystalline symbol shattered across the floor.

The sound of Legionaries kicking in doors and rushing inside distracted the dwarf little.

Yashin set his hand up to it and pushed. Nothing happened. He pushed a little harder and it started to move, pivoting slightly before getting stuck again.

"Imbert," Yashin whispered.

Turning his head slightly towards the boy, he saw an ever slighter nod.

"Stay outside the vault. Do not let the vault close before I return."

Without a soul noticing, his shadow slipped back outside the vault.

As the Legionaries descended the hall, they're enthusiasm died out. Kicking in doors faded away to merely opening them, and the teams entered cautiously rather than violently. Not a single soul cared as a single Legionary pushed the last door open in disappointment.

"There ain't nothing here."

'bAadrooOOoOon' the golem rumbled.

"Did you hear that?" A Legionary asked.

The Decanus began to reply, "Are you asked if I heard the-"

'BadROOON,' the golem cried.

"Do not cut me off, *thing*!" The Decanus yelled at the golem.

It was in the brief moment of silence Yashin heard a faint sound. Not far away, something quiet and airy. A torch, he thought in the moment. The sound snapped momentarily, closer to his ear this time, and with the faintest touch of warmth. He swatted at his side, and opened his mouth to chastise whoever was holding their torch so close to him, but there was nobody there.

Seeing this, the men stared upon him with a puzzled look.

"The draft spooked me," Yashin shrugged it off as.

An ounce of emotion finally coming back out in the form of shock, Justinian said, "The draft spooked *you*?"

"Are you all afraid to descend those stairs, is that what this is?" The Decanus questioned. He then jabbed Justinian with the tip of his Gladius and pointed the blade down the staircase.

The traitor dawdled down the staircase, Peuris hounds nipping at his heels. The golem marched on behind them without missing a beat, until it suddenly stopped in front of the prisoners at the first step of the staircase.

"The hell, move it!" Falnon shouted at it.

The golem rumbled in a strange, low way that Yashin had never heard from it before. It was so strange that it managed to stand the hairs on the back of his neck up. Yet the golem marched on, though it appeared somewhat hesitant to Yashin.

Twenty steps down they reached yet another hallway. Yashin barely set a foot down on the level as an Imperial unenthusiastically opened the first door. The man yelped like a pup getting its foot stepped on, lashing with his gladius at what lay within as he flew backwards straight onto his arse. The other Legionaries poised towards the door like vipers ready to strike.

The Decanus grabbed the man by the arm and yanked him back up. "Up you fool!"

The golem stood still as the inanimate objects that composed it, and the prisoners walked around it to get a peak at what was within the room. Hanged from the doorframe was a badly decomposed body, its now severed arm laid beside its feet that floated merely an inch from the ground.

"One dead body and everybody loses their composure. Well, are we here for men? Get to it."

The men start moving, but one after another each stops and looks around.

"What now?!" The Decanus puffs.

"Didn't you hear that?"

"The *draft*? You all are as bad as the nonhuman," he said, flashing a look at Yashin.

Splitting into two groups, the contubernium begins to search the mere zig-zagging three doors remaining on the level. The first group searched the next room in silence, and the second group busted into the third room moments after.

"We got more bodies," one Legionary shouts.

"More suicides," another clarified.

Yashin waddled his way over, the golem now trailing behind instead of marching mechanically behind the Imperials. At least a dozen corpses hung from the rafters of what appeared to be a grand dining hall. Grand tables ran down the room, empty platters offering only dust for the corpses. A great fire pit with grills and spit was located in the center of the room, above it great vaulting chimney leading only to a collapsed ventilation shaft.

"Boys," a voice called behind them. Yashin turned to see a Legionary leaning in the doorway. "There's… I don't know what this is… over this way."

Yashin began waddling towards them, but the Decanus rushed infront of him and pushed him aside. The five Legionaries present, as well as Falnon, trailed behind their leader—except for one who stopped with a sad look and let Yashin out.

Looking down the hall, the Imperials congregated around the final room as the three Legionaries of the other team emerged from within. Justinian lurked beside them and stared deeply into the room. The men exploded in a babel amongst themselves.

"This place is unholy."

"What the hell happened here?"

"What are we going to do now? Just keep finding bodies over and over again?"

"That ain't just bodies, Gnaeus."

Then a low rumbling noise caught Yashin's attention. The hair on his neck stood up once again as he turned towards the sound. The several moments the golem rumbled felt like forever, then it stopped. All of a sudden it started moving intently, walking past Yashin, then past the Imperials, and into that last room. Yashin followed it, the others too caught up in their jabber to notice the behemoth stalking past them. The golem stopped at the base of a tower of bones crushed and broken and packed into what first resembled to Yashin a great termite mound, then as a twisted human form. The Golem reached its large wooden hands into the tower and ripped a caved in skull from it. Yashin looked towards Justinian and was met with an alarmed stare.

Justinian began looking around with a confused look.

Then Yashin heard something. It was loud this time. There was a vague sensation of a voice speaking to him, but there were no words. Nor did it seem as if it were attempting words. Something was speaking to him, but it was not a being.

'ROOOoooOOaaaAAAAnnnnnN!!!'

Everybody's attention was now on the Golem. Its hand closed with great force, reducing the skull to a cloud of dust. It swung around with greater speed than Yashin thought an entity of such mass could; the Legionaries' torches danced about in the draft it created. Next thing Yashin knew the Golem was on top of him. He hustled out of its way, the Golem narrowly glancing him and knocking him backwards. The Imperials scattered to avoid the behemoth as it raced further down into the bowels of the vault.

The kind Legionary stumbled over to Yashin and offered him a hand off his back. Yashin would not take it.

"After it!" The Decanus shouted.

The Legionaries chased after it eagerly, descending the next staircase with raging torches. In their excitement they left behind the prisoners without care, even including Justinian. Falnon followed behind them nonchalantly, leaving Nurin, Yashin, and Justinian.

"I can't do this, Yashin, I can't!" Nurin cried.

"My friend, I have lived on for centuries. The boy Emperor is not getting me killed today. Do as I say and we will make it out alive."

Nurin nodded, albeit on the brink of tears.

Yashin pointed his crossbow at Justinian, and a moment later Nurin sheepishly did too. *'Maybe we won't die yet...'* He thought.

"Well? Go on Justinian, don't think all of us have forgotten about you."

The three then followed after the others.

Descending down the staircase, the walls gave way to a large open room. Pillars and arches and statues of strange figures were scattered across the room in various stages of construction, ancient scaffolding falling apart around them. An incomplete section of vaulted ceiling had collapsed in at some point, opening the room to an adjacent cave above. If Yashin had been able to feel the draft, he would have known this is the other end in which it originated from. And carved into the wall across this room was a large arching doorway, in which Yashin barely chanced to see the Golem running further into.

The men chased after it, the gap growing as they could not keep pace with it. As they passed beneath the collapsed section of ceiling, a large figure swooped down from the shadows above. Yashin did not have time to warn them. Fangs bit into the neck of a Legionary, ripping out their throat. Claws cut into the next before anybody could realise what was happening. There was a confusing brawl of swords and claws that Yashin could barely process as he raised his crossbow. Then a Legionary stuck a spear through the sail of skin spanning between the creature's arm and body. The creature struck the shaft of the spear with its claws and snapped it in half before lunging forward and ripping out the man's neck.

Yashin aimed for a Legionary and let his bolt fly.

A second bolt shooting past him caught Yashin off guard. The bolt then struck the creature right beneath its large, pointy ear, and the creature collapsed immediately. Yashin looked over to Nurin, who's normally worried face for once looked of pride.

Yashin looked back towards the men and was met with the Decanus storming up to him.

"You shot Gnaeus, dwarf!" He screamed in Yashin's face.

"It was an accident, Dekarchos." Yashin was glad the mask he wore hid his grin from the man. "I must confess, however, that my mistake pains me little."

The Decanus ground his teeth. "I will have your head for this."

"And Severus will have your head in return," Yashin reminded him. He doubted the Praetor would care at all if the Decanus *were* to kill him, but hoped it would be enough of a threat to keep the man at bay until he could take care of him as well.

"We'll see when we return to camp, filth." The man turned back to the men.

Three Legionaries stood among the fallen, visibly battered and waiting for some sort of command.

"Come on…" The Decanus said breathily as he marched on after the golem.

All the men followed him this time, including Justinian, and the two Dwarves worked on reloading their crossbows. But then Justinian stopped and turned back to the Dwarves.

"Where'd your little friend go?" He asked with a puzzled look.

Yashin pointed his freshly loaded crossbow at the men, "Get movin'."

As they walked forth behind the rest of them, Nurin pointed his crossbow at the ceiling and all over. Nurin was still a nervous wreck, Yashin found, but he seemed to have something more in his stride since killing the beast. Stepping over the bodies of the fallen, he studied the beast which had killed so many. It was part man, clad in dirty, torn clothes, but with the fangs, ears, claws, and wings of a vampire bat. Another beastman.

He wondered what lay further down into the vault. A minute later he would find out as he passed through the doorway.

On the other side lay a large, circular room with a huge cavernous ceiling, a U shaped pit encircled all sides of the room other than the entrance, leaving a large flat plain in the middle. On the far side of the plain were two thin spires of rock that reached twenty feet into the air, arching and twisting together towards the top. The room was not natural, yet it was clear to Yashin that it was formed, not built.

The golem stood in the middle of the room, trembling with its hands wrapped around its head. But as they approached the golem, nobody seemed to notice the figure kneeling down between the two arches across the room. Slowly it stood up, letting out deep breaths as it turned towards the group. It had the nose of a bull, horns, and hooves, but human arms, chest, and mouth. Not all the men noticed it until it roared half man, half bull.

The three Legionaries left scurried to a combat stance, spears and swords ready. Leading behind them was the Decanus. He opened his mouth to order his men, but before he could the beast jammed its fingers into its eyes. There was silence as it worked its fingers deeper into its eye socket before it ripped its eyeballs right out of its head. The Legionaries looked back and forth at one another, unsure what they were witnessing.

The beastman raised its hands into the air, a bloody eyeball in each palm. The eyeballs began to fly around the room, the flesh from within the socket trailing like a gruesome tail. The two little horrors flew around, studying the members of the group. It came up and studied Yashin, who cocked his head at it. After narrowly blowing past Yashin, it went up to Justinian and flew straight into his forehead. Justian lurched backwards in disgust, and the eye bounced back nearly a foot. It then rammed his face a second time.

"Fuckin' hell!" Justinian shrieked as he swatted at it.

The Decanus then impaled it with the tip of his Gladius.

The beastman immediately roared in pain and anger. With both hands, it reached down and picked up a greatsword that had been resting on the ground next to him.

"Kill the beastman!" The Decanus ordered.

The three Legionaries charged at it. The first one stabbed his spear at it, but the beastman glanced the tip away with the greatsword, slid its blade down the shaft, and impaled the Legionary. As the beastman drove its blade through the first Legionary's chest, the second one stuck it in the side with his spear. But the beastman was able to draw his sword from the man's flesh before the spearman could, and the beastman took the Legionaries' head off with a single swing of the greatsword. The last remaining Legionary charged at him with gladius in hand. The beastman swung upon him, and the man parried the blow, only to have the sword ripped from his hand and flung off into the nearby pit. His heart was then split into two as the sword was wedged into it.

"Justinian, I hope you're ready for a fight..." The Decanus asked.

The Decanus to the left and Justinian to the right, the two began walking towards the beastman, planning to flank around the left side of the golem . Yashin stood back as far as he could, Falnon not too far ahead of him. Nurin by his side up until this point, but now the Dwarf was creeping around the opposite side of the golem, crossbow tight in hand.

"Wait." Falnon spoke out. The three members all paused their advance and looked back towards him. He walked out between the two men and the golem. Standing right past the golem, he closed his eyes, laid his palms out ahead of him, and took a deep breath. Two balls of flame appeared in his palms, then he clapped his hands together to form one large ball of flame that shot out at the beastman. Mere feet away from him now, the beastman exploded in a flash of fire when hit by the ball. The men relaxed a little, and Falnon looked back with a smirk. Then the fire dissipated, revealing a charred yet still alive beastman heading right for Falnon.

He furrowed his brow as he saw Justinian and the Decanus tense back up. Looking over his shoulder, he saw the beastman still coming at him and attempted to run. He made it two steps before the greatsword was protruding from his ribs.

Yashin raised his crossbow and aimed it at the golem. The beastman was brushing shoulders with the golem when he let the bolt fly.

The bolt struck the crystal core of the golem with immense force, yet the bolt broke apart on impact and merely cracked the crystal surface. But just as Yashin could register how little damage his mighty weapon had inflicted, the entire crystal core was suddenly shocked with a web of cracks. Stunning rainbow rays beamed out of the cracks and rapidly intensified to a blinding white light. He knew what was next. Counted on it, in fact. As he dropped to the floor, a shockwave filled with grit, splinters, and other debris impacted Yashin harder than any wind from the Voron steppes could ever. While he may have evaded the worst of it, it did not spare him from all harm, for a chunk of shrapnel made home in the meaty spot of his right shoulder blade.

Even after the shockwave had passed, Yashin remained on the floor. It wasn't until after a few seconds when something squishy landed on his shoulder and rolled away that he slowly opened his eyes. Raising his head from the stone pillow, he looked through the glittering dust and at the once floating eyeball had now been torn to shred. Yashin made his way to his feet and evaluated the situation he had created. The Golem had been reduced to little more than debris scattered around the room and the dust in the air. Having taken the brunt of the explosion, the beastman was now a pile of shredded meat, guts sprawled several feet across the floor. The quickest onto his feet was the Decanus, now rubbing the dust out of his eyes and spitting the grit from his mouth. Justinian struggled to his feet, still alive but haven taken the greatest beating. Except, where was Nurin?

Retrieving his crossbow from the ground first, Yashin waddled over to the edge of the pit and peered down it. The fellow Dwarf's body laid at the gravelly bottom, twisted unnaturally and oozing blood. It was Humans who did this to his compatriot, Yashin thought. It may have penultimately been his hand that sent the bolt, but it was only because of *them* this had to happen.

Yashin looked away from it and to the men. The Decanus was now sticking the carcass of the beastman with the point of his gladius. Justinian had managed to find himself a large stick to lean on that had once been part of the Golem. In a lot of pain the Dwarf drew back the crossbow string and loaded another bolt. Then the strange noise whispered upon Yashin's ear again. He felt like it was trying to get at him, get in him. Squinting at something else that sat between the arching pires, he headed towards it. It was an altar of some sort and something was sitting upon it. As he grew closer he realised it was a face. It was a black mask carved in a menacing scowl. Dark red lines were painted from the eyeholes to the bottom of the mask, resembling tears of blood. He could sense it was something powerful, something malevolent, something he should not mess with.

Turning around and waddling towards the doorway, the Decanus called after him, "Where are you going, Dwarf?"

He continued leaving as he replied, "Back to camp. I think we have seen enough here, don't you agree?"

"Dwarf…" the Decanus grumbled.

Yashin waddled his way straight back to the surface, the Imperials limping after him. He found it almost just now that the oppressors were now reduced to his level in some way. He went across the great hall, weaving around the deceased, and up the first set of stairs, then across the hallway, up the second set of stairs, and across the hallway again. At first Imbert was nowhere in sight, but as he drew close the man made himself seen. When Yashin passed through the vault door he listened to the footsteps behind him. One was not too much farther than him, and the other was falling behind.

"Close it," Yashin ordered Imbert.

Feet behind him, the Decanus began screaming at the top of his lungs, "Duh-woooor-"

Yashin cut off the Imperial's hollering with a bolt through the throat. The man's body fell forward near instantly, his head laying contorted in the doorway. Imbert pressed in the centre stone and the door began rolling shut again. Justinian started moving quicker, grimacing from the pain. Then his leg gave out, sending him topping into the floor, and adding a cracked skull to his list of injuries. He forced his way to his feet, but once there he did not move. He merely glared at Yashin, a sheet of blood running down half his face.

Yashin stood on the other side and waved just before the door slammed shut, trapping Justinian inside.

◇ Chapter Ten

The sun was setting fast. The sky above their heads was black with clouds, and the horizon to the west barely a sliver of skyfire. Despite being almost in complete darkness, they knew they were coming close to the compound. But as the sun rapidly set within minutes, Yashin noticed something alarming—the sunset was not the only thing on fire.

"Do you see that, Imbert? Or are these damned tinted lenses playing tricks on me eyes?" Yashin whispered, worried that beastmen may not be far.

Yashin had to look back at his shadow to see him nod.

The two continued creeping through the woods for several yards until they reached the deforestation line. Hiding in the bushes they looked across the field of stumps and at the compound. The palisade sat unmanned, not even by any fallen Legionaries. It was charred and falling apart, but this was only from the battle prior and bore no new damages. Behind the walls the compound burned, but there were no sounds of battle, no screams, nothing but the quiet crackling of the fire.

"This doesn't appear to be a beastman attack," Yashin told his compatriot, knowing not to expect a response. "I suppose the only thing we can do now is go see what happened and hope we don't find ourselves in too much trouble."

Yashin trekked out of the bushes and headed across the barren field. He didn't like leaving himself in the open, but by the compound design there was no other way. At least it was night and the clouds blocked out any light from the sky. And by the time he reached the gate nothing had surprised him.

All was quiet inside the gate as well. With his right shoulder injured, he kept the crossbow readied with his left arm. His arm was getting quite sore too. He wasn't used to holding it one handed, let alone in his off arm. The duo headed towards the foghouse. It wasn't long after that they finally came across the bodies. Prisoners and Legionaries lay dead in the streets. Even more corpses likely resided in the now burning bunk houses. Then they started coming across different bodies as well. Men in civilian clothing yet not prisoners of Mancipus, all with axes and swords and various other weapons strewn beside them, a few clad with helmets or gambesons. Yashin's suspicions as to the identity of these men grew as he approached the Foghouse. Flames consumed the roof and bursted out of the windows. In the light of the fire he could clearly see the massacre of his men, the strangers, and a few Imperials. Then he saw one completely different figure laying face down in the dirt with their skull bashed in from behind—one of his girls. He kneeled down beside her and rested his crippled right hand on her shoulder. Even though she was a human she didn't deserve this violent end.

"Yashin…" A familiar voice groaned.

The Dwarf turned towards the voice. It was Borivoj, slumped against the stoney wall of the burning tavern. Yashin had just thought he was another dead body until now.

"I led Krolik right to you," Borivoj confessed in his native Voron tongue. "I did not intend to…"

Yashin waddled up to him. "I know you didn't."

His man's eyes shut halfway as he grunted weakly.

"Is Krolik here, Borivoj?"

Borivoj laboured to speak, but no words came out. He gave up trying and his head slouched defeatedly as he pointed towards the Castrum.

"Imbert…" Yashin called upon.

He needed not say more than his name. Yashin turned his back just before his shadow pierced Borivoj's heart with his dagger.

With his man put at peace, the Dwarf made for the Castrum. It was time to confront his long running nemesis Krolik.

The gates of the Castrum were swung wide open. Very strange, Yashin noted. Inside the courtyard were predominantly dead Imperials and only a couple dead thugs. Whatever happened here must have taken the Imperials by surprise. The two crossed the quiet courtyard, stepping over the bodies. On the other side, Yashin threw open the door into the grand hall. On the other side two of Krolik's thugs spun around, but it was too late for them. Yashin sent a bolt straight into one's chest, and Imbert sliced open the throat of the other before he could react. Atop the gallery, an orchestra of swords clashing played, and the cries of both sides sung alongside it. But what Yashin cared about more was the long haired, bushy bearded man standing in the centre of the hall watching the symphony.

Yashin quietly gestured to Imbert to go around the colonnade. When the boy was hidden away, he threw his crossbow to the ground and shouted, "Krolik!"

His adversary turned his dead, nearly white eyes to Yashin. He replied in the Voron tongue; "Ahhh, Yah-sheen. I thought you had fled again like the roach you are."

"Why fight and die when I can give you hell from a distance?" Yashin spat.

Krolik drew a sword from under his black cloak and began towards Yashin. "Finally nowhere left for you to run, stuck on this island. If only these Flouvs knew the monster they had right here…"

"Oh Krolik, you have been too preoccupied with me to notice the monster in your own shadow…"

The man stopped, but did not take his eyes off Yashin. "What does that mean?"

Imbert emerged from the colonnade behind him, gliding across the marble tiling like a ghost. He didn't know Imbert was there until the blade was in his spine. Imbert caught him by the neck as he collapsed and guided him to his knees.

Yashin unravelled his face wrapping as he walked towards the squirming, half paralysed man. Getting inches away from Krolik's face, he grinned as he told him, "I would say see you in hell—but, unlike yourself, I will never die."

The squirmed less and less til all was still. Yashin was somewhat disappointed—he wanted to see the life in Krolik's eyes go out, alas they were soulless to begin with. He sighed.

"Drop him. We got him, my boy."

Imbert smiled. Yashin smiled. *So eager to please, the poor lad is*, Yashin thought. He ripped out those girls' hearts for his drunken father's approval, only for the man to turn him in to the authorities. Then to be transformed into a weapon for the local governor, only to be tossed away and thrown into the dungeons when Peuri's Imperial audits began. But Yashin would not be the next one to let him down.

The cacophony in the gallery above became riddled with confused shouting, and turned from fighting to running. Four thugs spilled down the staircase from the gallery and fled the Castrum. Severus calmly came down after them, Spatha and Pugio in either hand, and covered in blood—of which not a drop was his.

"Damn Vorons," Severus muttered, sheathing his blades. "Did you take care of Justinian, dwarf?"

"Yes we did," he answered.

"Good." Severus commented.

"What now?"

"Now I shall return to the Empire, and then rid the world of the boy Emperor."

Yashin and Imbert glanced at each other with uneasy eyes.

"Well I don't take it you two have much love for the Emperor, do you?"

The two shook their heads.

"No. We do not," Yashin affirmed.

"I don't care about you, one way nor the other. As far as any shall be concerned, no prisoner survived the Mancipus colony."

◈ Chapter Nine

The pile of bones and rust that were once a Flouvern Decanus laid on the cold stone floor of the vault, untouched but by time. Suddenly the hall of the vault began to rumble and vibrate. The massive door began to screech and roll open. As the door struggled to open again for the first time since Yashin sealed it, the vault shook and shivered erratically, the Decanus' remains shifting about. The door finally slammed into its final position, and everything went still. Then a pair of leather boots gracefully stepped over the Decanus. And behind them came an entourage, stepping on his remains and kicking them across the vault.

The red man was amazed that after all this time the Dwarf still held onto the combination. He was apprehensive what if anything this all would yield, as everything Yashin told him was from a millennium ago. The vault's door was attacked by picks and pry-bars and all other kinds of tools, but it appeared that all attempts to breach the vault had been unsuccessful. Whether or not the mask was still there, he was unsure. He and his men continued descending the vault.

They wasted no time, ignoring the rooms along the hall and straight down the stairwell. As the red man neared the bottom, he saw a pair of long, furry ears poking out from around the corner at the bottom. Then a pair of dark, humanoid eyes slowly appeared and watched him. The eyes quickly retreated behind the corner again, it's ears still sticking out. A few steps later they crept out again. And then the creature hid its whole self back around the corner. The red man took his last step down the stairs and turned towards the creature. It had the shape of a humanoid—a dwarf he would assume from its height—but the ears of a rabbit, big bucked teeth, whiskers on its cheeks, huge elongated feet, and a patchy fur coat. The two merely stared at one another for several long seconds; until the beastman let out the most horrendous screech. The red man winced at the sound and backed up. The creature ran deeper into the vault and his men started to chase it.

"Leave it!" He commanded.

The men stumbled to a stop. Twitching and whimpering, they looked at the red man in fear, and then back towards where the beastman fled like rabid dogs.

"Leave it," the red man commanded them again. He was tired of these wild beasts. He had broken down and dominated their minds, but this left them violent, erratic, and dysfunctional. The mask should solve these issues if it had the power he had come to think it to. Yet so little was known about it—it was scattered crumbs of a legend, scarce to even the greatest of arcane knowledge, seemingly unseen for a millennium. But he was certain it had all the power he thought; he had spent most of his life on this quest. And then he would have the perfect men serving him.

Further into the depths they continued. They passed through everything Yashin had told them, through the unfinished room and past the skeletal remains of the dead Legionaries, and through the grand doorway into the domed room Yashin said the mask would be. To the red man's surprise, there was a figure standing in the room, and it was not the rabbit-thing.

It wore Legionary armour above its coat of thick brown hair; it held a gladius, not in hands but in great claws. Hearing the men, the fur stood up on the back of its neck. It then loudly sniffed the air. It spun around, revealing its long bear-like snout, raging eyes, and six swollen nipples poking out of the rusting armor. Its eyes swelled with anger as it roared like a bear. The red man thought it almost sounded like it screamed, "Peuri".

The bear-man came at the red man, fast yet with a bad limp.

The red man raised a hand to signal his men to stay back and drew his sabre with the other. Calmly he stepped towards the charging bear-man.

When the two reached each other, the bear-man flailed its gladius at the red man, and he calmly raised his sabre to parry. When the gladius met the sabre, it shattered into shards like glass, and the shards continued to break down in a cloud of dust. The bear-man spun to the side and stumbled, and the red man took the opportunity to slash halfway through the back of its knee. Half its body collapsed to the ground and it roared in pain. Propping itself up on its other knee and arms, it tried to swing at the red man with its claws, only to get it chopped clean off with another swipe of the sabre. The red man then put his foot between the bear-man's shoulder blades and pinned it to the cold, hard ground.

"Yashin sends his regards, Justinian," he told the beastman.

The monstrous Justinian's eyes widened with rage, only for a moment later to narrow lifelessly after his vertebrae were severed by the tip of the red man's sabre.

Procuring a rag from his red coat pocket, he wiped the specs of blood from his face then his blade. Returning the rag to where it was, he looked across the great domed room to the strange arching spires. It was once a doorway between worlds used by the Elves, but now a tear in the fabric of existence; a bleeding scar from the fracturing and collapse of worlds called the Convergence; an oozing hole between this universe and the Darkness. The red man could not just feel it, but see it whereas nigh others could not. And sitting right in it was the mask, just as Yashin had said. This mask was strange though—it was not an object imbued with Eldritch magic, nor the natural magic power of this world as the mages and druids and Elves harness—but something different, yet nonetheless immensely powerful. And in combination with the tear between universes, it was an unbridled chaos reaching for anything it could and warping it into chaos.

And the red man took hold of it.

He put it up to his face and let his mind meld with the relic. He could feel the power of it within himself—for anybody else the sensation would be overpowering, but years of meditation, discipline, and practice in the arcane kept him unfaltering. He could feel all the life around him—or more strangely, it was more so feeling the slow fading away of life.

"Come," he commanded the rabbit-thing.

And it, in a trance, came to him.

The red man looked through the hellish vision of the mask and into the creature's very being. Within were two entities amalgamated together, a Dwarf and a rabbit, screaming in torment. He stretched his arms out towards the creature and placed his palms together. His fingers twisted and bent and kneaded before violently throwing his hands out. And then the two were disunited.

The Dwarf rubbed his head as he spoke in Dwarven, "What horrible nightmares…"

"They are over now," the red man replied in his tongue.

The short humanoid stared at him with surprised, bloodshot eyes, "Who…who are you.?."

"I am a friend of Yashin. You are Nurin, I presume?"

"Ye-yes..? What happened?"

"Several centuries have passed. The Three Empires have collapsed. The mask seems to have kept you alive as a beastman, as you called them."

"Mask? Wha-... Wa-wait, I was a be-beas-beastma-.?!" Nurin looked down to the lifeless corpse of a rabbit next to him.

"Yes."

"Wh-why is he dead but not m-me?"

"You sustained severe injuries during the raid of this Temple, when I separated you I was able to heal you using its lifeforce."

Nurin slowly nodded his head as if he understood.

"Unfortunately your dark brethren seemed to believe you had perished. He has undoubtedly moved on and back into the shadows." The red man removed a hefty pouch from his pocket and tossed it at the Dwarf, who—rather than catching it—ducked in fear. "Inside that pouch is more than enough Richters and Stone to get you back to the mainland. The neighbouring island has a village with a port that sometimes has ships from the mainland; I can take you there and no further."

◈ Epilogue

Goreg sat at an open window of a mighty tower reading a scroll, the sun warm on his leathery green skin, but the gentle breeze kept him at the perfect temperature. His finger tracked under the letters at a snail's pace struggling yet determined to read the text. Suddenly a small creature grabbed him from behind, wrapping their gentle arms around his chest. Long chestnut hair draped over his shoulder right before soft lips kissed his neck. Goreg smiled, closed his eyes, and lifted up his hand to caress the sweet creature. Then he groaned and slumped over.

"What's wrong Goreg?" the sweetest—to Goreg at least—voice asked as the creature wrapped itself around the green behemoth.

Goreg looked over to his mate—a human woman, whom most might describe as homely, but in his eyes the most beautiful one in the world—and spoke with sadness. "Lost place."

"I'm sorry love. Might a kiss make it up to you?" She asked with a cheeky smile.

Goreg smiled. "Suppose."

The two shared as passionate a kiss as a human and a large green monster could, before she wandered away. Goreg squinted at his text as he tried to find his spot. Finally he found where he left off. '...*profundum inferni...*' But before he could continue on, a drop of water landed at the tip of his finger. He looked up from his text to a raging storm. Suddenly the wind was blowing fiercer and colder than any storm he had experienced in the summits of the Makrag Heights. But it was the torches of approaching armies that made the hairs all over his body stand up.

He jumped up from his chair, knocking it over as he spun around. But the Legionaries were already storming into his room.

"Here he is! There's the creature who has been holding me and my daughter hostage!" A man shouted.

"Lucius?!" Goreg asked horrified.

"Father no!" The beautiful maiden shrieked.

"Silence!" Lucius commanded his daughter.

"What in hell are you doing?! Goreg no!"

"I said silence!" He screamed.

Tossing herself at her father swinging at him, she screamed, "Stop them!"

The Legionaries surrounded Goreg with spears and swords. The green giant stepped back from the men, almost tripping over the chair. Lucius grabbed his daughter by the wrists and pulled her in tight. Through the discord of the soldiers shuffling around and making beastly noises towards him, Goreg could hear his father-in-law whisper, "You are going to get us all killed. I'm sorry, my child."

Knowing what he must do, Goreg fell onto his knees and put his hands in the air, and prepared himself to die.

He woke up as he felt the Legionaries chain him up.

Goreg laid in the bushes of a temperate forest, the sun warm on his leathery green skin, but the gentle morning breeze made him feel a little chilly. He looked around in fear, but seeing nothing crawled out of his bush. First matter of business, he relieved himself on a nearby tree. Then he went onto his second matter, finding and picking Cloudberries to tame his hunger. Munching on the berries, he watched the distant smoke still plumbing a week later. He felt a small sense of guilt in running away when the Vorons attacked. Not for his Imperial captors, but for his fellow prisoners whom were slaughtered. Yet he had never killed a man—nor any other intelligence creature—and he would never do so.

Knowing he would be executed if the Praetor survived the attack and he was to get caught, he decided to go back to camp. The giant smoke signal made the many mile journey back to the camp easy. Seeing no activity at the gates, he made his way into the smoldering camp and found the only life was the swarms of flies feasting on the dead. He had a quick meal of pickled asparagus and fuzzy bread before wandering aimlessly around the camp. Eventually he came upon the flagpole behind the Castrum, the colors of the Empire still flying proudly over its ravaged colony. Goreg unsheathed his knife and did what any intelligent creature would—carved into the pole: *Goreg was here*.

Appendices

____

The Three Empires

Our tale begins at the birth of time itself. Long ago, before man was born out of dust, there was a mighty race that traversed the stars, wielding power far beyond anyone's comprehension. They lived freely and without bounds, exploring the universe and the lands beyond. Despite their vast amount of power and wisdom, this ancient race failed to see the seeds of destruction they left behind.

This ancient race travelled inter-universally and was able to explore and interact with fantastic places and beings. However, the transportation they used to get from one universe to the next left holes and weaknesses in the very fabric of the universe. It is said that a few of the wisest scholars of their race realised their folly and pleaded with their brethren to cease their excessive expansion and exploration throughout the multiverse, but their cries fell on deaf ears.

Eventually the structure between the universes began to collapse causing cataclysmic effects. The seams between these separate worlds began to tear. There was nothing keeping the universes separate. At first, many of these ancient beings rejoiced in what they thought was the merging of reality. However, this merger was the precursor to apocalyptic destruction.

As universes began to overlap, the laws of physics and nature began to conflict and worlds began to crumble and burn. The ancient race was shocked and many sat idle while those who predicted this event took action. These brave souls rapidly began closing the gaps between the universes, many giving their lives to do so. The ancient race only barely held reality together, but it came at great cost. Things from foreign universes became trapped in others. This convergence, as it was later referred to, left so many beings and monsters stranded in unfamiliar landscapes and the once mighty race that traversed the stars was trapped in all corners of reality. Unable to reunite, they too were stranded as monsters in hostile and unfriendly environments.

*****

In our world, we Humans were oblivious to this foreign invasion. We were so early in our development as a people, we believed these monsters and races had always been a part of our world. Humans lived in decentralised, nomadic tribes that roamed the world like leaves in the autumn breeze. There were no kings or priests to restrict and oppress men, only the dangers of the environment and the instinct of survival.

Soon tribes would begin to encounter each other and have territorial disputes. Out of these disputes alliances were born and the first tribal federations began to emerge. However, borders were never established and fealty was fickle. These federations never achieved much but bloodshed. It wasn't until Rhimond Llewod of what is now considered Kovera rose to power within his federation, that true government was formed.

Rhimond began by implementing military standards that had never been used before. He would have his warriors train and practice before allowing them to fight in battle. This made his army far more formidable than the loosely organised bandit gangs that most other tribes used as a military. Since Rhimond had superior military strength than his neighbours, he conquered them. He established himself as a despotic monarch and laid formal claims to the region surrounding his capital.

Rhimond's aggressive expansion caused other tribes around him to form their own governments and reform their militaries. These reforms spread quickly throughout the world reaching even the far west. However, the far south never would adapt to these reforms and remained as nomadic tribal nations for many centuries to come.

These newly installed governments brought about the age of kingdoms, however each region expressed their governments in different ways. This era was fraught with war, bloodshed, poverty and famine. This highly unstable and volatile time was one of great border fluctuation. Borders would shift so much, Kingdoms would be forced to move their capitals and lose their old capitals. The cultural differences between sub-regions was not enough to facilitate a large enough resistance to foreign governments, so there were few partisan issues within kingdoms.

After many centuries, these warring kingdoms finally came to peace when one government overcame the rest within their cultural regions. The Kraftvollenriech to the north uniting all of the Krafts; the great Flouvern empire in the south governing the Flouvs, and finally the vast Empire of Voronia to the west uniting the isolated Vorons. Thus began the age of empires.

*****

The Empire of Voronia was a very loosely bound group of Voron tribes. Their monarch, whom they called a Tsar was selected from a pool of champions representing the individual tribes of the empire and the last one standing was crowned emperor. The tribes were extremely autonomous, the only authority of the emperor was during war and arbitrating internal disputes. The Vorons maintained their warlike stance as the other empires developed into more political and economic maturity.

The Voron terrain and landscape was harsh. Winter ravaged all hopes of warmth and lasted through the majority of the year. In the majority of the Empire of Voronia, the ground rarely ever thawed in the summer making agriculture impossible. The villages relied on hunting and fishing to feed themselves. Due to the vastness of the land available within Voron territory, when a village got too large to feed, the elders of that village would simply half the population and send them to start a new settlement with more game. After hundreds of years the population, though no census was ever taken, was well into the tens of millions making the Empire of Voronia the most populous empire by far.

Though a time came when the abundance of game that had always been available started growing scarce. Villages tried to downsize further, but there was little territory left to expand into. Many local administrations tried different tactics to resolve this food shortage, but since there was no organisation between regions, it had little effect. Eventually famine spread throughout the empire and Vorons died in the hundreds of thousands. Villages would completely depopulate in weeks, leaving thousands of ghost towns strewn across the empire.

It was this catastrophic famine that inspired the current emperor, Pishche Voyna to take action. Before the famine, Voyna had started to build an army that was loyal to him alone and not the tribal leaders. It was this military that he used to wipe out all of the elders and chieftains and replace them with officers from his ranks. As he restructured Voronia, many young men joined his regime seeking food and favour. After a mere six months, Voyna had eradicated all of the relevant tribal leaders and placed Voronia under a military regime.

With this absolute control over the people, Voyna ordered rationing and his soldiers received priority which further incentivized joining his regime. He had civilians begin clearing massive amounts of lumber and constructed war machines and selling the rest to import grain. Soon, the military might of the Empire of Voronia was superior to the other two empires combined. Voyna led his army to the western edge of the Flouvern empire and razed all of the border towns and cities. He sent a diplomat to the Flouvern capital demanding that all borderlands within five hundred miles of Voronia be ceded to him immediately. The Flouvern emperor refused and led his army out to meet Voyna, but was shocked to see the might and vastness of the Voron military and then agreed to Voyna's terms.

Voyna slaughtered all remaining Flouvern citizens and immediately populated the area. He had massive farms built and those borderlands became the breadbasket for the rest of the Empire of Voronia allowing the population to grow once more. The government would send grain to all regions who would distribute it to towns. However, soon after the conquest, Voyna fell ill, many believing him to be poisoned and died suddenly.

The succession of this new militarised government was undetermined and Voyna's second-in-command quickly seized power before anyone else had the opportunity to. Despite his legitimate claim, Voyna's second-in-command was assassinated only a few hours after seizing power and the son of Voyna, Skuchny, took power. This instability, despite being brief, weakened the administration enough for the autonomy eager regional governments to push for power. Skuchny had no choice but to allow for the increase in autonomy, but he was able to force the regional governments to pay tribute in order to fund the military. Thus the position of emperor once again lost its power over the empire, the true power resting in the autonomous states that made up Voronia.

*****

The Flouvern empire was a mighty and progressive state in the central south of our world. It was the birthplace of reformation, both culturally and theologically. It started in what is now the Eidirium empire.

Several republics were spread across the shores of the Marmedius sea, these republics remained independent for many decades after the formation of Voronia, but were eventually forced to become a confederacy with the increasing border friction to the north and east. With war on the horizon, the Flouvern Confederal Congress made up of representatives from each of the smaller republics, elected a commander-in-chief to lead and organise the military. The first man elected to fill the role was Virez Inunitatis. Receiving pressure from the Federal Congress, Virez started a campaign to conquer the surrounding kingdoms, in what is now Trevalle. Many of these unstable states, also seeking protection from the north, surrendered and joined the Confederacy of their own volition.

The expansion of Confederacy under Virez continued north until they bordered the Krafts. The entirety of the Marmedius sea was surrounded by the great Flouvern empire. However, expansion came to an abrupt halt when Virez died from an apparent suicide, though none know why and many assumed he was assassinated, but the Federal Congress never had the issue investigated. Virez was not replaced due to the lack of potential expansion, and the Federal Army was disbanded, forcing the local republics to start their own militias and militaries.

It was around this time when the Church of the White Sun was founded in the Kingdom of Eidirium. A prophet claiming to have been blessed with a message from God while exploring deep into the Southron realms began preaching and telling people to turn to the Sun or be faced with eternal damnation. Many people flocked to his teachings and soon he was speaking before hundreds of thousands of people who thought he could perform miracles and would alleviate their pains and burdens. The theology spread like a wildfire throughout the Northern realms and with no opposing centralised religion there was little conflict. In Eidirium, King Seraphicus Paternarum publicly professed his faith to the Sun and gave power to the church's clergy and within weeks, made it mandatory to follow the Sun. It was here where the first inquisition was born.

Soon after this enlightenment period, the Empire of Voronia declared war on the Flouvern empire, which despite its superior technology and tactics, was too unorganised from the dissolution of the Federal Army to properly defend its borders from the seemingly never ending flood of Vorons. The Flouvern empire lost much of its borderlands, a very fertile part of the empire. The Federal Congress was outraged and immediately reinstated the Federal Army with Seraphicus as the Commander-in-Chief. Seraphicus was very ambitious and used funds from his own kingdom to further the army beyond its intended size and power. Seraphicus gave martial authority to his officers in his own kingdom, allowing them to be a police force. Soon he would press other republics and kingdoms into allowing his soldiers to police their lands. This was brought before the Federal Congress as an invasion of rights, but Seraphicus claimed he was enforcing federal laws on the corrupt lesser states and with his silver tongue, managed to be licensed to use the Federal Army as a police force in all states, being able to overrule the lesser governments and their militias and law enforcement.

The Federal Army soon began to press local militias into the army through fear and bribery. When many of the lesser governments had relinquished their soldiers to the Federal Army, Seraphicus lobbied for the Federal Congress to ban all decentralised militaries and armed groups, making the Federal Army the only executive power in the entire Confederacy. This outraged many of the larger nations in the Confederacy, who threatened to secede from the Confederacy if the Federal Army was not restricted. However, Seraphicus was able to table the proposal in Federal Congress and by the next day, many countries had seceded from the Confederacy.

Concerned of appearing weak, the Federal Congress was convinced by Seraphicus to make secession illegal and a bill was passed turning the Flouvern Confederacy into the Federal Union of Flouvern States. This gave Seraphicus justification to declare war on all the seceded countries, who were brought swiftly back into the Union and their local governments eradicated. Seraphicus took control of these states, leading them through a military regime. Knowing his power was growing, Seraphicus formed his own political party that he forced the administrations of smaller countries into by strategic assassinations and fear tactics. Soon he had more than half of the Union under his thumb and forced their representatives in the Federal Congress to vote for his agenda. In six short months, Seraphicus had the Federal Congress vote to dissolve itself and give supreme power to the Commander-in-Chief of the Federal army and immediately declared himself Emperor Seraphicus the Unifier, Divine Sovereign of the Flouvs. This officially formed the Flouvern Empire.

In the decades following Seraphicus' reign, the Flouvern Empire grew to be the leader in technology and philosophy. Many of history's greatest scientists, theologists and philosophers thrived during this time period commonly referred to as the Pax Flouvernum, where all countries thrived both economically and culturally.

*****

The Krafts have been a people of war for as long as people have recorded history. Their history begins in anarchy and wide dispersion. The rich lands of what is now the Olfenreich were filled with individual patriarchies living together with little contact with other families. These family units were very territorial and blood feuds were common over disputed land, because land was the only measure of wealth.

Women were treated like property in this early society. The only use of a daughter was to trade with other patriarchies for their land or rare luxuries. The men lived with their fathers and on their father's land for their entire lives, while women were sold off at ages as early as five or six and lived with their husbands' family for the rest of their lives. It was also common for women to be traded even after childbirth because there was no binding ritual like marriage in this society.

The Krafts lived in this dispersed anarchal society for thousands of years with little change. Even after the centralization of other regions, the Krafts still lived like they always had. Foreigners who visited Kraft lands could not see past what they thought was barbarism and dismissed the land as a wasteland similar to the Southron Realms and never sought to invade or influence the region. The great Flouvern emperor, Seraphicus led his army to the Kraft border, looking upon it he said, "Inutilem terram," useless land, and turned his back to it.

During the years of the Pax Flouvernum, the Kraft region went through a massive reformation. In the recent centuries, the Kraft patriarchies had slowly been growing bigger which pressed each patriarchy to acquire more land, but there was only so much. Eventually the patriarchies started to eradicate each other and take their land for themselves. During this time only the strongest patriarchies survived.

The leader of the foremost patriarchy noticed that many of the patriarchies were dying out and all of their history and culture that made each one unique was being lost. At first, this didn't bother him, but as the years went by he saw the destruction of so much of his people's heritage. During a war between his patriarchy and another, a large portion of his family was killed, including many of their story tellers and historians— who were the only recorders of their past—were killed. He soon realised that this was happening everywhere in the Kraft region. This disturbed him deeply, theorising that soon the entire Kraft population would lose its identity or worse, destroy itself.

The Patriarch Albrecht von Clausich summoned the elders of the patriarchy and raised his concern to them, who laughed and dismissed his fear as a foolish womanly thought. To the elders, the thought of their patriarchy being the only Kraft civilization was appealing and felt natural to them. This reaction frustrated Albrecht who sought to find support in the people of his clan. He would send messengers to influential members of the patriarchy and explain his concern, but none took it seriously.

Albrecht, who was running out of options, thought that a costly war might make his people realise the urgency of the situation, so he declared war unexpectedly on a neighbouring patriarchy. The battles were bloody and little was gained. Albrecht refused to press advantages and intentionally provoked unnecessary battles. The war ended with white peace, but both sides paid a heavy price. However, Albrecht's hopes were not met. The cost of war was lost on his people who had become so desensitised to violence and what they considered as a defeat only fueled their thirst for blood.

There was nothing Albrecht could do to sate his people's thirst for blood and achieve peace. He had no other choice but to do the unthinkable: diplomacy. He reached out to an ancient branch of his patriarchy that split off many centuries ago. To his surprise, the patriarch, Frederick von Wizten, shared his fears and agreed to meet in secrecy. Albrecht was extremely eager, but was cautioned by his closest friend and greatest advisor, his brother, to expect a trap. Albrecht heeded his brother's advice and took an armed regiment to the meeting. When Albrecht arrived at the meeting spot, a sandbar in the middle of a river that served as a border, he left his guard on the river bank and when Frederick came, he had also brought a guard and left them on his side of the river.

The two, Albrecht and Frederick, met in the middle of the sand bar, both a bit uneasy, but embraced each other like brothers. It was that first handshake that led to the unity of the Kraft people. The two talked for hours and long into the evening. They discussed everything from politics to personal matters. It was refreshing for both of them to speak to someone outside of their family and outside of their experiences. Albrecht knew that if he could find common ground with an outsider, all of the patriarchies could.

For months the two secretly corresponded, planning their scheme to unite their two patriarchies as an example to the rest of the Krafts. It took years to convince their respective families to be open to the idea of meeting outsiders. Albrecht started with his closest friends and advisors, who spread the idea to their closest friends and after nearly a decade of this dispersal, the general populace of both patriarchies, von Clausich and von Witzen, agreed to the proposed merger and during the final years of the Pax Flouvernum for the first time in Kraft history, two families shared a meal at the same table united as the Clausich-Witzen patriarchy.

This new patriarchy was far more powerful than any of the other families in all of the Kraft region and under the guidance of Albrecht and his second, Frederick, the Clausich-Witzen patriarchy started influencing the other patriarchies to come to peace with their brothers and reconcile their differences. They enforced peace throughout the Kraft region with their far superior armies and brought many warlords out of power, replacing them with younger, more diplomatically open leaders. However, despite Albrecht's best efforts it still took many generations to finally bring the Krafts to peace. Though he never saw the Krafts come to peace with each other, he did say before he died, "The Krafts will rise together through the unity of brotherhood and rule the world with the expectations of family."

While the Krafts were resolving their blood feuds, the Flouvern and Empire of Voronia were trading blows, constantly fighting over the Fertile Lands. Each side grew more powerful with each battle implementing the cutting edge of technology in warfare. During this time, the Flouvern Emperor decided to investigate a way to invade Voronia from the North. He sent scouts to find a path through what he thought was the barbaric wastelands of the Kraft region, expecting the scouts and his manoeuvring to go unnoticed by the primitive Krafts. However, his scouts were completely outwitted and captured in the unfamiliar Kraft terrain by some common Kraft hunters. The scouts were brought before the local patriarch who referred them to what had become the informal higher authority, the Clausich-Witzen Patriarchy. The current patriarch, Albrecht's grandson, questioned the men, who pleaded to be released and asked permission for their emperor to move troops through their land. The Patriarch sent one of the men back to deliver a message to the emperor, he kept the other imprisoned. Surprised by the sophisticated response of the Kraft leader, the Flouvern emperor agreed to the proposed parley.

The Patriarch and the Emperor met at a mutual site on the border, much like Albrecht and Frederick did so many years ago, but this time it was not so peaceful. The Emperor was deceitful and sly tongued. He sought to use the Krafts as a weapon against Voronia, but the Patriarch was no fool and saw through the Emperor's scheme despite the difficult language barrier.

Infuriated, the Flouvern emperor ordered the invasion of the Kraft land and he pressed his generals to move quickly, giving little time to plan and prepare. The invasion was a bloodbath for the Flouvs. They moved through unfamiliar terrain and fought an unusual enemy with foreign tactics. The commanders of the Flouvern army had no idea how to fight the Krafts, who had no centralised defence or army. Eventually, for fear of exhausting his manpower reserves, the Flouvern emperor called off the invasion and turned his eyes back towards the disputed lands.

This foreign invasion raised many questions in the Kraft region. The patriarchies held a convention to discuss the pressing issue. Many people believed nothing needed to be done, while others thought there must be a retaliation and even others who thought that they needed to centralise. The conference lasted many months with the patriarchs fighting over what they thought was best and in the end it came to a vote and the patriarchs voted to elect an absolute Emperor and form a centralised country made up of the patriarchies who declared themselves principalities. It was decided that at the death of every Emperor, a new patriarch from who were now called Princes would be elected Emperor. This effectively formed the Kraftvollenreich, which did not take an official name until much later.

For centuries the Clausich-Witzen family reigned as emperor. Their Principality was the greatest of them all. The Emperors led the Kraftvollenreich to great prosperity and dominance on the world stage. The Pax Flouvernum ended when the Krafts declared war, claiming the lands of modern day Bordreaux. This war ended with decisive victory over the Flouvern Empire, shocking the world. The Krafts asserted themselves as the dominant power over both the Flouvern Empire and Voronia, taking large amounts of territory from both.

During the expansion of the Kraftvollenreich, the head of the church in the Flouvern Empire, the Pontiff of the White Dawn, decided to take action. He ordered thousands of missionaries to enter the Kraftvollenreich and start evangelising the heretics. A majority of these missionaries were killed and sent back in pieces, however a few were successful in converting small groups of Krafts. One of these converts was an influential member of the Clausich-Witzen family, he approached the Emperor and tried to get him to see the light, but the Emperor refused, naming him a traitor and exiling him from the Kraftvollenreich.

Sparked by his kinsman, the Emperor of the Kraftvollenreich ordered a purge of these infidels, claiming that the Old Traditions were the true way. However, by that time one of five Krafts were following the White Sun. This persecution caused great unrest and the new followers of the White Sun started to come together and their numbers grew daily. In months the number of White Sun followers outnumbered those of the Old Tradition, the people who held the power. Noticing this, the Pontiff of the White Dawn sent support into the Kraftvollenreich, arming the White Sun followers.

The leaders of the White Sun followers soon formed a coalition against the government and declared war, throwing the Kraftvollenreich into a civil war. It was a long and bloody war with brother fighting brother, family against family it was more devastating than any other war the Krafts had ever experienced. It ended with the surrender of the Emperor, who was forced to abdicate the throne and executed for his crimes against the White Sun and the White Sun was made the official religion of the Kraftvollenreich.

The princes elected a White Sun Emperor, but not of the Clausich-Witzen dynasty. This Emperor, Inbicollutus von Whittelensichzen, who took an Eidirium name in honour of the White Sun, welcomed the church into the Kraftvollenreich. He worked very closely with the Pontiff of the White Dawn to institute church authority in the Kraftvollenreich. Churches and cathedrals were built all over the Kraftvollenreich and the people were extremely zealous, eager to embrace this new faith. Bishoprics and Archbishoprics were instituted under the authority of Inbicollutus. However, this focus on the church was slowly destabilising the country. Economic growth and development were at a standstill. Trade routes were left absent. The pleas of the people fell on the deaf ears of a preoccupied government.

Famine spread throughout the Kraftvollenreich and the people were angry. The government had become paralyzed by their focus on the church. The Flouvern Empire took advantage of this by allying itself secretly with the Empire of Voronia and doing a surprise attack on the Kraftvollenreich. This was a swift and crushing war resulting in the slaughter of millions of Krafts, civilians and soldiers. The war ended in the liberation of the Aurillac region and the northern Voron territories. This war would later be known as the Magna Bellum.

Outraged by Inbicollutus, the Princes forced his abdication and was sent into exile. The Princes of the Kraftvollenreich felt betrayed by the church and quickly purged it of its role in Imperial affairs, but still remained zealous followers of the White Sun. It took the Princes many months to elect a new Emperor because many families were lobbying for the throne. During this time, three distant Principalities declared their independence consolidated under one King who held the three titles. This would become known as the Westkaiserreich and Szolnok, who would consider themselves Krafts, but still different enough from the rest of the Kraftvollenriech to want their independence. The Kraftvollenreich was in no place to enforce unity, but instead reelected a Clausich-Witzen Emperor who brought stability to the empire. He gave more autonomy to the Principalities and dissolved the Kraftvollenreich into the Olfenreich, in honour of the split Kraft culture. With stability restored, the Olfenreich grew into a world power once more, leading the world in technology and economic prosperity.

*****

In the last years of the Pax Flouvernum, the Flouvern empire, which was locked between the Kraftvollenreich to the north, Voronia to the west and the endless lands of nomadic Horselords to the south, decided to look beyond the Northern Realms. The Emperor at the time, Invenio Expiscor sent hundreds of ships out to sea on exploratory missions. Most were never seen again, but a few came back with findings of the fabled Eastern Isles.

No Northerner had ever landed in the Eastern Isles and come back to tell the tale. The stories that surrounded the Isles were scary to say the least. Many people believed the Isles were inhabited by tribes who practised Dark Magic and would eat their own comrades. Others believed that the Isles are the source of monsters and demons that plague the world. Despite all this, Invenio wanted every opportunity to get an edge over the growing threat to the North. He dispatched exploratory regiments to scout and map the island.

Six months later, shattering everyone's expectations, the entire crew—save one who died of infection—returned. The explorers reported that there was a large native population, who were surprisingly docile and were only slightly inferior in technology. Though they were unable to establish proper communication, the native hosts were gracious, giving them gifts of gold and spice.

Under the direction of Emperor Invenio ordered the acquisition of the Eastern Isles. The invasion was almost bloodless. The native people seemed to either be welcoming or oblivious to the foreign invaders, the only rebellious clans being in the North. This occupation led to a symbiotic relationship between the Flouvern and the Easterners. The Flouvs mined for gold and harvested spices, while the Easterners were taught about new technologies and quickly converted to the White Sun once the language barrier was broken.

Before the Flouvern Empire could fully integrate the Eastern Isles, which was called the Celenthrand Isles by the natives, the Kraftvollenreich became hostile. After the annexation of Aurillac, the Krafts also occupied the Celenthrand Isles. Even after the Magna Bellum, the Celenthrand Isles stayed under Kraft control. The Krafts were a much harsher overlord. They set up military installations all over the Isles and forced their own government on the natives. It wouldn't be until much later that the Celenths would earn their independence.

*****

Despite the Voron and Flouvern attempts to destroy the Kraftvollenreich during the Magna Bellum, it simply lived on, albeit slightly reduced, as the Olfenreich. The Voron Emperor signed a peace agreement with the Olfenreich Emperor, stating that the Vorons no longer had any interest in Kraft territory. This infuriated the Flouvern Emperor, whom in his outrage declared war on the Voron Empire, claiming the Fertile Lands as his own. The brief war ended with the loss of all Flouvern holdings in the Fertile Lands and thousands of casualties on the Flouvern side.

This defeat started widespread opposition to the Flouvern Emperor. His legitimacy was questioned by many influential members of the Flouvern empire. Only six months after the defeat, a massive coalition formed within the Flouvern empire against the emperor. This coalition aimed to force the Emperor to abdicate and replace him with a Commander-in-Chief, reinstating the Federal Union of Flouvern States. However, the Emperor who refused to abdicate, with what little supporters he had, was able to cripple the national government by assassinating many key figures and burning most of the government's records and documents. At the eventual defeat of the Flouvern Emperor, the coalition decided to award independence to all Flouvern states and dissolve all ties to the Flouvern Empire, Union, and Confederacy, returning the Flouvern region to its original form.

The Empire of Voronia continued long after the dissolution of the Flouvern Empire. The Voron emperors continued to fight over the disputed Fertile Lands with southron horselords and the newly reestablished Eidirium Empire. However, soon the support for the Fertile Land conquest decayed among the northern and western Vorons. They no longer felt it was worth sending their young men to fight someone else's war. These groups simply refused the drafts and then soon refused to pay tribute to the Voron emperor. Then the kingdoms began to break away from the Empire of Voronia, until it was no more.

This was the political scene for the following centuries, with little changes in border or relation. To the far west resided the Voron kingdoms, whom simply survived and continued expanding into the unknown western lands and fought with the south and east over the Fertile Lands. To the north, the Olfenreich continued to prosper, but paralyzed on the international stage by its many internal political issues. In the remaining south east laid the Flouvern land, who spent much of their time praying and crusading against the endless hordes of Horselords in Southron Realms in hopes of one day finding the Holy Land. This leaves the Celenthrand Isles, who will go on to eventually gain their independence from their Kraft oppressors and write their own pages in our history books.

To Kill The Crocodile

I ground my teeth to stubs as I watched my comrade, my friend, beaten by the officer from under my dark hood. It was brutal. The sound of the whip cracked through the square filled with silent, mostly human, onlookers. With each cry of agony from the elf, my brow hardened. Between a lash the officer turned to the crowd and screeched like a gore bird over its prey,

"Let this be an example to all humans of how elves are seen in the eyes of the Flouvern!" He spat in the wounds upon his victim and brought the whip back down.

My body trembled with fury as I stood powerless to save my brethren. Sweat beaded at my brow and lip as the heat of my anger became more and more palpable. I glanced at the sky, the sun not yet at its highest, but nigh noon.

Back on the relentless beating, my gaze fell. My brother's back no longer looked elvish. It was bruised and torn. They had not the mercy to gag his mouth, thus blood ran from his lips where he had bitten his tongue. What was left of his trousers was torn and tattered while dyed crimson in his own blood. What was once an elegant mane of hair now resembled a greasy rat's nest filled with dirt and grime. This once beautiful creature of nature had been reduced to a wretch by another, equal creature.

A cry of agony rang out in the square as the whip was brought down for the last time. I winced at the pain of my brethren as the whip broke across his back. The officer threw the now tattered and bloody whip to the ground beside the pulped elf. From a rack he drew a great axe and gripped it tightly in one hand. In horror, I watched as he drug the limp elf from the whipping post across the square to a chopping block. The elf was tossed to his knees, his neck strewn across the block.

I glanced up at the sky again, the sun at its peak. Again, I looked down to the scene. I watched the officer boast at his accomplishment and brandish his axe. He raised the axe above his head in preparation to swing. In a flash if flung the heavy folds of my cloak from around me, revealing a warbow in my hands. I drew the notched arrow and loosed it, the arrow flying towards its target with precision. The officer fell to his knees, an arrow planted in his forehead.

The square erupted in chaos. Civilians ran from the plaza and the other hooded figures shedded their outer shells, revealing around twenty well armed elves. Imperial guards began to plow through the frantic crowd to reach the elves.

I grinned and notched another arrow, letting it fly into the breast of another guard. I

discarded my bow due to a lack of ammunition and drew a short sword. I darted towards a

another soldier, intercepting him at great speed. I ran him through with a simple slice of the throat while still maintaining my speed. I quickly rolled around, very agile on my feet, and grounded the blade into the gut of another guard.

With a hefty kick I dislodged my sword from the soldier's torso and scanned the scene. More imperial guard percolated into the square, but were being met by my comrades. I sheathed my sword and sprinted to the block where my brother was lain. I lifted him over my shoulder and trotted towards one of the plaza's exits where I was met by a group of five, rather angry guards. With a wave of my hand they fell to the ground, blood trickling from their ears; brain haemorrhages are quite painful.

I staggered, suddenly out of breath. For a few moments I was overtaken by a wave of nausea, but then I continued down the road at a brisk pace, recovered. My comrades loosely followed behind me as they dispatched their targets. Most of them replaced their cloaks around them, but I was hindered by my load. Slipping through the shadows and alleys we exited the city.

"That was risky and foolish, you inconsiderate, impulsive boy!" a much older elf scolded. "Too many things could have gone wrong. What if there had been more guard than anticipated?" he argued. "If one of you had been killed, our cause would be that much weaker." He shook his head and paced around the small study. "You need to start thinking about the potential consequences of your actions before you act."

"I saved our brethren. It was worth the risk." I said bluntly. "With all due respect, I think saving lives is paramount. If you want me to stop these missions you will have to detain me." I met the elf's gaze. "The way I see it, we have two options: you detain me and lose another soldier, or support me and save lives and recruit more rebels."

The man sighed. "Yovrne, you are hard headed, but you are passionate. I cannot afford to lose you, but I'd appreciate it if you did not threaten me so. I am still your commander. You have my blessing to continue your operations, but please consult me first."

"Thank you sir." I said with an inclination of my head.

"You are dismissed."

I looked around the room at my comrades. Each were sitting behind a small desk in a smaller chair. The room was poorly lit, but there were many charts and maps hung on the walls. They looked weary, but I began my speech nonetheless.

"The Flouvern is too vast for us to take on alone one to one. We must slowly infiltrate and destroy. Thus, we need to begin recruiting human supporters, perhaps relatives or old friends. Contact those you might think would consider. We'll have them brought here for questioning."

"There are several supply caravans passing through the area. Our spies have identified them as troop resupply and tribute collection caravans. They will be at their weakest point tomorrow, crossing the river. It is then where we will strike and plunder. Prepare yourselves for these will not be lightly guarded wagons. It is likely we will face upwards of one-hundred-fifty men." Grunts and murmurs whispered throughout the room. Some men grinned and others frowned while some shook their heads.

"The commander and I have been discussing a plan. We intend to make a very public action to inspire our brethren to rise against the empire with us. There is not much more I can tell you about the mission now, but only a few of our best will be selected to participate." I glanced around their faces watching as they did the same.

"That is all, you are dismissed."

*****

I sauntered down the road trying to be ambiguous, blending into the human masses. The sun sunk into the horizon upon the hills north of the city. Shadows began to stretch into the streets, masking the nooks and crannies of metropolis. I took a sharp turn into one of these havens of darkness. Crouching behind a few crates of mouldy potatoes, I scanned the street before me. Townspeople commuted to a fro. Merchants led donkeys hauling large loads upon their backs or pulling carts.

A hand pressed against my shoulder, I turned around quickly, a knife slipping from my sleeve and pressed it against the stranger's neck. I looked up to see my lieutenant, Jarven.

"It's just me!" he exclaimed, throwing his hands from under his cloak.

"Don't sneak up on me so, not with the tension in the air." I retorted, relaxing my knife. "Get down, the caravan will be coming through shortly."

We both crouched behind those crates for the many hours that followed. The sunlight faded from the sky like a shade being drawn over a lamp. The commuters that had previously filled the street had vanished, leaving them empty and barren. Our only company was our thoughts. We continued to sit silently, faithful that our target was coming.

The moon reached its peak and I sighed audibly. I stood up and struck the crates before me with my foot in rage sending the potatoes flying into the street. I curled my fists into balls and slammed them against the alley wall.

"Damn fools we are." I spat, "They changed the route. Our leads were false."

"Calm down!" Jarven chided, "We wish not to be discovered." He sighed and placed a hand on my shoulder reassuringly. "Come now, there will be other opportunities. The emperor moves around more than people think."

The sun rose over the city as I sat with a cloak pulled over my face, its shadow shielding me from prying eyes. Morning commune commenced and the town began to fill with merchants and peasants alike. From my perch I could see all the happenings in the square. I shook my head as I watched a procession drag through the plaza.

A long line of chained elves marched bare through the square. Their bodies were beaten and bloodied. Soldiers marched alongside them and beat them with whips and batons with no provocation. Peasants lined the streets screeching insults and taunts at the abused. I felt my stomach turn at the sight of the injustice.

My anger would not be sated. Too long the elves have suffered the injustices and treacheries of humans. Too long have they been powerless to fight back. Soon we will not have to live in the shadows. Soon we will live free with our human companions, colleagues, and compatriots. There are those who welcome the elves. Our society can be changed, we just need to give it a little push.

*****

"Was infiltrating the palace really the best idea?" Jarven murmured. "It seems a bit impractical."

"It could wait no longer. Tyreus IV must die."

We padded through the dark corridors of the palace under the veil of midnight. Even the clouds aided in our plight. Moving from corner to corner, we slowly progressed through the palace armed with only daggers and black cloaks.

Four and twenty we have already felled. The halls become more populated as we near our target. Only thirty paces more and six more laid dead. Our small unit would not be stopped this night. Generations of torment and abuse incarnated themselves in our stride. With the backing of all of our brethren we marched on.

The walls that lined our path to vengeance gravitated from plain grey stone to elaborate gold masterpieces accented with tapestries and paintings. The doors to the emperor's sleeping quarters stood not one-hundred paces from us. Between us stood our greatest obstacle: the imperial guard. Five and seventy men stood before the doors. We must kill all of them without arousing alarm.

I sit and cross my legs neatly beneath me. Casting off my cloak I pressed my palms together and closed my eyes. My comrades did similarly. I was one in a circle of five and as the last of us closed his eyes, we joined hands and a gleaming circle was inscribed around us, channelling our power into a conglomerate weave of spells.

We stood after our preparation was complete. Drawing our short blades we charged into the fray, cutting the first line of unexpectant men down. I drew my sword across a soldier's exposed neck, crimson droplets covering my garb. I rotated on my feet driving my blade through the eye of the next. With a wave of my hand the next line fell. I gasped for breath, my vision blotched. I staggered another step and rose my dagger as if it was lead to parry a desperate soldier's strike. A snarl formed on my lips as I drove it into his gut.

My comrades covered me as I struggled to recover from my exertion. I paused to listen, but heard nothing. I grinned, our spell had worked. Even as I pressed my foot into the wound of a dying man his screams I could not hear, nor could anyone else in this, the palace of the Crocodile.

It took us but to the count of eight score to slay the rest. The last soldier stood at the door with an uncustomary weapon. He wielded a great axe, brandishing it in the dim torchlight. I snarled recognizing the man. We stared at each other and we understood each other.

I sheathed my dagger within the folds of my cloak. Stretching my hand out towards him, my face contorted in anger. My fury possessed me. I screamed, but I heard it not. I turned my palm up and clutched my fingers into a claw. Turning my palm slowly towards the man, I drew my arm back and thrust it violently at him. He flew back against the door and I held him there, not caring about the drain of energy. I stalked closer, each step a generation of torment. My arm strained as I applied pressure to his skull. His face contorted with agony, but his cries fell on no ears. After a few long moments his skull collapsed and his limp body fell to the floor.

I flicked my hand lazily and the massive golden doors flew into the grand room behind them, crashing into the furniture and destroying the decor. I staggered into the room, my comrades behind me. We stalked towards a grand canopy bed. Behind the veils slept soundly the Crocodile.

We ended the spell containing the sound and I spoke venomously.

"Finally, Crocodile, I have the pleasure to meet you." I bowed mockingly. He looked up from his slumber startled, gripping the edges of his sheets, his eyes darting to locate something.

"H-how did you get in here?" Tyreus stuttered, resolving to stay still rather than run.

"Enough, Crocodile." I chided. "Your palace stands empty, your guards slain." One of my comrades lifted a severed head skewered on his dagger. "You are alone."

Composing himself the emperor straightened his back, turned to the side of his bed and stood, wrapping his nightgown around him.

"What is it you want? Gold? Land? Power? Women?" he scanned my unit with wary eyes. "There are plenty of things we can discuss."

"You would not make such a gracious offer if you knew who we were." I spat back at him. "Nor would we accept it from someone who has caused so much pain." I paced in a slow arc around the emperor. "You have forced the destruction of so many lives. There was so much opportunity stolen from those innocent people. You target them, beat them, discriminate them. Why? Why do you do it, Tyreus? Why?!" My voice rose to a yell and then to a scream. Tyreus seemed unphased by my accusations.

"Impure, filthy creatures." he mumbled. "There is no place for you in this world. You invaded us, I am merely exterminating the pest."

"Pests?" I screamed. "We have done so much for you! We watched you develop from the foolish apes that you were." I threw a vase from a table and it shattered against the wall. "You have no idea what our ancestors did for you!"

Tyreus remained stoic. He didn't move from his position. Pursing his lips he spat in my direction.

"I don't care."

*****

The sun rose, lighting the dark town. Humans and elves began their daily commutes. Passing through the town square they were met by the shocking sight of Tyreus' decapitated body hung by the feet from the statue of his predecessor. His head sat upon the chopping block only a few feet away. The Crocodile had been slain.